Coming for Christmas

Holiday Pact Book Two

Lizzie B Brown

Contents

This one is for all the naughty little smut lovers out there. Santa may not have your gifts, but I do. Enjoy.

Content Warning

This book contains sexual acts in public places, blow jobs at inappropriate times, free use, mentions of eavesdropping on others having sex, and other various sexual acts. There are also mentions of parental abandonment.

Mental health is important. While not everyone needs content warnings, there are those who do. You can find the most up to date content warnings on my website: https://www.lizziebbrown.com/content-warnings

Playlist

1. "Green Christmas" - Barenaked Ladies

2. "The Christmas Song" - Paul McCartney

3. "Little Saint Nick" - The Beach Boys

4. "Last Christmas" - Wham!

5. "Winter Wonderland / Don't Worry Be Happy" - Pentatonix (feat. Tori Kelly)

6. "Christmas Tree" - Lady Gaga (feat. Space Cowboy)

7. "Silver Bells" - Harry Connick Jr.

8. "Wonderful Christmastime" - Paul McCartney

9. "Carol of the Bells" - Straight No Chaser

10. "All I Want for Christmas is You" - Mariah Carey

11. "What are you Doing New Years Eve" - The Head And

Listen on Spotify: https://spoti.fi/48WMeWQ

Santa's Naughty Little Bar Crawl Drink List

Recipes By Jessica Furniss

Cockin' Around the Christmas Tree

8 oz white wine

2 oz white cranberry juice

2 oz club soda

One tall sprig of rosemary

1. In a highball glass add about ¼ inch of water and place a tall sprig of rosemary in the center. Carefully place the glass in the freezer, checking to make sure the rosemary is staying in the center as it freezes.

2. After the water in the glass with the rosemary is completely frozen, pull the glass out to make the cocktail.

3. Into the highball glass with the rosemary add the white wine, white cranberry juice, and club soda.

4. Serve immediately!

The Naughty List

2 oz Brandy
3 oz Eggnog
½ tsp Ginger powder
Sprinkle of nutmeg
Whipped cream
1 gingerbread man cookie

1. Add all ingredients to a cocktail shaker with ice and shake for 30 seconds.

2. Strain into a coupe or martini glass.

3. Garnish with whipped cream and a gingerbread man cookie.

Lick o' the Peppermint Stick

1 oz vanilla vodka

1 oz peppermint schnapps

2 oz heavy whipping cream

Whipped cream

Garnish with crushed candy canes

1. Add the vanilla vodka, peppermint schnapps, and heavy whipping cream to a cocktail shaker and shake vigorously for 30 seconds.

2. Strain into a coupe or martini glass.

3. Garnish with whipped cream and crushed candy canes.

Comin' Down My Chimney

2 oz bourbon

1 oz cranberry juice

½ oz lime juice

½ oz cinnamon syrup

Garnish with a cinnamon stick and star anise.

1. Add all ingredients to a double old-fashioned glass.

2. Fill with ice.

3. Garnish with a cinnamon stick and star anise.

4. Optional: add a cinnamon sugar rim by rubbing the lime around the rim of the glass then dipping the rim into a cinnamon sugar mixture (2 tablespoons sugar, ½ teaspoons cinnamon).

Whipped on Christmas

1 packet of hot cocoa mix

3 oz hot water

2 oz Irish cream

Topped with boozy whipped cream

1. In a heated mug combine the hot cocoa and hot water and stir until dissolved.

2. Stir in the Irish cream.

3. Top with a large dollop of the boozy whipped cream.

4. Garnish with holiday sprinkles and a drizzle of chocolate syrup.

Boozy whipped cream recipe:

1 cup heavy whipping cream

2 tablespoons powdered sugar

1 tablespoon Kahlua (or any coffee liqueur)

1. Combine all ingredients into a chilled metal bowl of a stand mixer.

2. Beat the mixture until stiff peaks form.

3. Chill until ready to serve.

Prologue
Alone in a Crowded Room

Nixon

Christmas Eve Fourteen Years Earlier

Nothing is more awkward than sitting in a room full of strangers. *And this is only the beginning,* I thought to myself.

I raised my hand to my face, absentmindedly pushing my black-rimmed glasses back up the bridge of my nose. It was such a common action that I barely noticed when I did it, but being nervous made me painfully aware I had adjusted them no less than five times in the last few minutes. I needed to get my shit together.

This was only Christmas Eve—a small, intimate gathering of nine people, including Poppy and me. Tomorrow's Christmas lunch was the main event. The house would be bursting at the seams with people by noon, if Poppy was to be believed. Tonight was only the immediate family—her mom, stepdad, four siblings, the eldest's partner, and us. At least I wasn't the only non-blood relative tonight.

Why did I let her talk me into joining? The thought plagued me as I wiped my sweaty palms down the legs of my jeans as inconspicuously as I could.

I could barely handle this small crowd. How was I supposed to deal with a packed house tomorrow? Normally, I didn't have social anxiety, but this was Poppy's family. I couldn't exactly drown my nerves with booze until Fun Nixon came out to play.

You wouldn't be alone if you indulged a little more, I tried to convince myself. Hell, I'd probably fit right in.

Mr. Smithfield, her stepdad, was on his third beer of the evening, and I lost count of how many glasses of hard cider the other adults had drunk. Not that you could tell by the way they were acting. Everyone seemed to handle their alcohol really well.

Thankfully, Poppy was nursing her glass, though that had more to do with the fact that it was spiked with rum and she was in a tequila phase. *Thank god Christmas margaritas aren't a thing.*

The only people not drinking at all were the two youngest—Fallon and Zane. Though Zane definitely had his eyes on the others' cups, like he might swipe one if left unattended.

I was the odd man out in a room full of conversations. Sitting on the corner of a plush gray couch, I silently took in my surroundings. Even Kim, her older sister's girlfriend, looked more at ease than I felt, talking with Fallon and Zane.

Anyone on the outside looking in would instantly know that I alone was the stranger among the family. It made my stomach twist in knots as I silently prayed for an excuse to leave.

Not that I had anywhere to go or any way to get there. Poppy drove us the three hours to her parents' home, where we were staying in the guest room. The best I could do to escape was excuse myself to bed, which would definitely raise a few eyebrows. No, I was stuck here until the evening's festivities drew to a close.

Poppy sat next to me, deep in conversation with her younger brother, Jacob, about college life and the girl he started dating. My attention was only half with her, the rest of my brain focused on smiling and not staring at my hands as I fidgeted.

Maybe I should fix a drink to help me relax.

Everyone was so warm and happy, a concept that was still fairly foreign to me. Yeah, I got a peek at what a loving family looked like after my parents kicked me out and Jack's parents took me in, but I had almost eighteen years' worth of cold, distant holidays molding my view of the world. All the laughter and holiday cheer felt weird. I doubted that would ever change.

"So...what's the story with you two? Moving in with a guy after only a few months doesn't seem like you," Jacob said, pulling me back into their conversation.

His voice was light as his eyes sparkled with mischief. There was no doubt what he was actually asking, but the reality couldn't be farther from the truth.

Okay, maybe he wasn't that off in his assumptions. In the five months I'd been living with Poppy, we'd fallen into bed together a few times, but on an emotional level we hadn't moved past friends. Not that I would complain if things progressed into something more. It would honestly be a dream come true.

The first moment I saw Poppy at that convention a couple of years ago, I was a goner. I had no idea who or what Sailor Jupiter was, but it didn't matter. She took my breath away. There was something about her that drew me in. I needed to be in her orbit always.

Unfortunately, I didn't make the same life altering impression on her. Not even my thwarting some pervert's attempt to get up-skirt shots seemed to impress her. She wasn't cold or anything, quite the opposite, but I wasn't able to hold her attention the way she held mine.

That pull to her never went away, not fully. Even when I was dating Ginny, I still felt it. Maybe that's why I ended up on Poppy's doorstep when my relationship with her friend fell apart. I told myself, and her, that it was because I had nowhere to go, but that wasn't true. I could have always gone back home and crashed with Jack until I was on my feet, but I hated the idea of going back there and depending on him again. So I followed the Siren's call and ended up in the last place I expected to be.

She invited me to crash on her couch and nursed my wounded heart. In the end, the breakup was a blessing because it brought me closer to the person I actually wanted, even if it wasn't in the capacity I hoped. Not that I was going to admit any of that in front of her brother.

Poppy cackled at Jacob's question. There was no other way to describe the comical sound that burst from her. It hurt that her response was so immediate and dismissive, like the idea of us together was nothing more than a joke. Despite the ache in my heart, I kept a smile plastered on my face. Deep down, I knew she wasn't trying to be mean. If the past five months taught me anything, it was just how much she cared.

"No, no. Nothing like that Jake-y," she said, wiping away a tear. "Nixon's not some random piece of dick. He's my bestie."

A bittersweet warmth filled me. I was more than some random piece of dick, I was her bestie. She'd never called me that before. I always thought Sophie was her BFF, but somehow in the last few months I had taken that spot...and I didn't even know it happened.

Jacob nodded slowly, his eyes darting between us like he knew there was more to the story but wasn't sure what.

I offered a shrug and a crooked smile, desperately hoping the conversation would change course. I didn't make a habit of inviting strangers into my personal life, making the current situation a mini-nightmare, even if I was thrilled to find out I was Poppy's bestie.

Poppy's mother huffed, drawing our attention to where she sat with Mr. Smithfield and her eldest daughter, Amy.

"Language, Poppy! We have guests," she scolded.

I fought back a chuckle while Poppy rolled her eyes, her mother's pleas having no effect. That felt like such a Poppy reaction. She was unbothered by the admonishments of others, unwilling to bend to their will. It was one of the many things I loved about her.

"This isn't Kim's first Harper-Smithfield Holiday, and Nixon doesn't care," she argued back.

The matriarch gave me an apologetic smile, her eyes silently pleading for forgiveness. It was strange how little she looked like Poppy, or I guess how little Poppy looked like her.

Unlike Amy and Jacob, who were the spitting image of their mother with blonde hair and blue eyes, Poppy took after her father. It was a point of irritation for her made worse by the fact that the two youngest looked like their father, with black hair and grayish-blue eyes, making her stick out from the rest. I had no idea what that felt like, growing up an only child.

"Be nice to your mother. Please," I whispered, feeling the need to defend her mom.

Mrs. Smithfield was nice, much warmer than my own mother. Ever since we arrived, she'd been bending over backwards to make me feel welcome in her home. I wanted to tell Poppy how lucky she was to have a place to go home to, filled with loving parents, even if Mr. Smithfield wasn't her "real" dad. The only thing stopping me was the risk of having my own past exposed. It had been a few years since my parents kicked me out, but I still choked back tears anytime I tried to talk about it.

Poppy gave me a look of faux outrage, pulling her hand to her chest as she scoffed. *Always with the dramatics.*

"Et tu, Nixon? Really?" she said in a mocking tone.

"Poppy, stop," her stepfather warned. "You didn't drag this poor boy here to make him uncomfortable among strangers. Your mother raised you better than that."

"I really did, I swear," her mom added with a hint of snark, making me smile.

***

After letting myself indulge in a few glasses of the warm, rum-filled cider, I felt more relaxed. Probably because it was barely more juice than alcohol. At least it took the edge off enough that I was able to open up a little more around the others.

Their family dynamic was a curious one. Amy, being the oldest by a good ten years, appeared to be more distant from her younger siblings. At first, I thought it might be because the two youngest didn't share the same father as her, but the way she spoke to Mr. Smithfield, occasionally referring to him as Dad, quickly nixed that theory. She spent most of the evening conversing with her parents, while the other siblings had formed a tight huddle around the couch.

"When she left for college, she never moved back. Only visits for holidays and such," Poppy whispered.

"Huh?" I mumbled.

"You keep glancing at Amy. She's not avoiding us, she's just not as close to Fallon and Zane due to timing. She left for college like a week or two after Zane was born. It's nothing personal, just the gap in age."

I nodded along like I understood, but I didn't. I was an only child, and all my friends who had brothers and sisters were all close in age. Poppy's family was a different story entirely, though.

Amy was the oldest at thirty-three, with Poppy coming in second at twenty-three. Jacob, the last child that their mom had with her first husband, was twenty-one. Fallon, seventeen, and Zane, fifteen, were products of their mom's current marriage. Eighteen years between the oldest and youngest was definitely a gap.

"Amy thinks she's too adult for us. That's why she's sitting with Mom and Dave. Give it another few minutes, and Kim will wander over, though. She knows who the cool crowd is," Jacob added.

I stared blankly at him for a beat, trying to figure out how to respond. There was clearly a hint of hurt feelings over their sister sequestering herself with the adults, but none of them were actively trying to include Amy, either. I couldn't help but wonder if this was what sibling rivalry looked like.

"So, we like Kim more?" I said.

It came out as more of a question than a statement, but the smile on Jacob's face said he didn't notice, or didn't care.

"Exactly," he replied, slapping me hard on the back.

The friendliness was escalating in a violent way. It made me think about Jack's childhood stories of wrestling with his older brothers, and the bruises that sometimes decorated him. He wore them as a badge of honor, proof he could hang with the big boys. That was great for a ten-year-old Jack, but not a twenty-three-year-old Nixon.

Poppy flashed me an excited smile, pleased her brother was warming up to me. I knew when I accepted the invite to join her how important it was that her family loved me.

Family was everything to Poppy. It stemmed from her own trauma growing up. Trauma that she was all too eager to share at great length, unlike me, who bottled up my past. The end result was a tight relationship with a group of both blood and found family. When we signed the lease to our place, she excitedly exclaimed that now I was officially family, too. At the time, I was happy that she was happy, but now I felt a bit overwhelmed by the crowd.

"I need to refill my drink," I said, eager to separate myself from the group for a moment.

Everyone gave me a nod, except Zane, who asked if I could grab him some as well.

"You're fifteen, no," Poppy scolded firmly.

The youngest sibling scowled back at his sister as he huffed in frustration.

They were nice, all of them eager to make me feel welcome in their home. Even the distant Amy, who chastised Poppy for speaking on my behalf when their mom offered to fix my first plate of food. It was so strange, but I couldn't deny the warm glow that filled me here, even if it was a bit suffocating at the same time.

Standing, I paused long enough for the floor to stop swaying beneath me. *Probably should switch to water.* Thankfully, the ground beneath me stayed solid as I ventured into the kitchen.

My thoughts drifted to the Christmases of my childhood as I searched the cabinets for a fresh glass. The overly formal attire, the suffocating boredom, and the constant reminder that children were barely to be seen let alone heard. I hated the holidays for so long because of that.

It seemed silly to complain about it considering how absolutely spoiled I was. Coming from an overly wealthy family meant I got everything I asked for and then some, but even the gifts weren't about me. It was some weird competition my parents had with their friends. I figured it out when I was fourteen. My mom kept asking if I'd shown off any of the fancy electronics I'd been given, some of which I hadn't even asked for. Suddenly, even the gifts were tainted.

"Nixon, sweetie? Are you okay?" Mrs. Smithfield's soft, southern drawl called from behind.

I jumped and spun around, cheeks red. I had done nothing wrong, but I still felt like a child caught with their hand in the cookie jar.

"Um, yeah. I just—water. I mean." I paused, sucking in a breath. "I was going to switch to water. Just trying to find the glasses."

Mrs. Smithfield stood silently, her eyes carefully assessing me. It was only a few seconds, but it felt like an eternity as her gaze bore into my very soul. It had been so long since anyone had looked at me, really looked at me, the way she was. I wanted to crawl in a hole and hide, terrified she could somehow see the scars I was hiding.

"The cabinet to the right of the sink," she said, finally breaking the silence.

Her lips curved into a soft smile as she walked over to the cabinet in question and grabbed me a glass. I let out the breath I was holding, relieved the strange moment had passed.

"Here you go, hun," she said.

She offered the glass to me, and I accepted with a mumbled thanks, not quite sure what to do with the dirty one.

"You don't have to be so nervous, Nixon. Despite what my daughter might have said, we don't bite. She might, but we don't," she teased with a wink.

I chuckled nervously, unsure if she actually knew that her daughter did indeed bite. My cheeks flushed as I pushed back the unwanted thoughts of Poppy in the throes of ecstasy, sinking her teeth into my flesh. The last thing I needed was a boner while talking to her mom.

"It's not that. It's just—" I didn't finish my thought, not wanting to unload my past on a stranger. Talking about my parents would definitely kill the festive mood.

"Nixon." Mrs. Smithfield grabbed my chin, holding me so she could look me in the eye. "I'm not going to say whatever happened to you doesn't matter. That wouldn't be fair. And I'm not going to force you to talk about it. Just know that you are home now, okay?"

I swallowed the lump in my throat as I struggled to process her words. We'd only just met, yet she could see right through the façade of a man to the broken little boy. And she was offering me a place to call home.

Like mother, like daughter.

I didn't know this woman, but her offer pulled me in. All I wanted was to be loved. That's probably why I was so quick to jump into a relationship with Ginny. It was also why I didn't hesitate to accept the invitation in front of me now.

"Yes, Mrs. Smithfield," I said, fighting back tears.

"No, no, no," she said, releasing her hold. "That's far too formal for my taste, dear. Call me Fran."

I nodded, unable to hold back the smile on my face.

"Okay, Fran. I can do that," I said.

"That's a good boy. Now, get you some water and rejoin the group. It's about time to open our Christmas jammies," she ordered.

Our what?

Chapter 1
Christmas Eve Morning

Poppy

Christmas Eve Present Day

I let out a long yawn, stretching my arms above my head as I begrudgingly roused from sleep. Being awake was overrated, dreams were so much better.

Last night's dream was the best. A very sexy red-headed hacker boy with glasses from my favorite Otome game came to life and showed me just how talented he was with his hands. I was seconds away from coming when I suddenly woke, humping the body pillow decorated with his image. *Great.*

With a huff, I pushed the pillow off my bed and turned to face my very real nerd-boy roommate in hopes he could finish what my dream started...only he wasn't there.

What the fuck?

I hadn't woken up alone since the day before Thanksgiving. He'd been taking full advantage of our little holiday pact for the last month, using it as an opportunity to get all the morning cuddles. While I'm not normally the biggest cuddler, I don't mind making an exception when those cuddles regularly become something more.

Throwing the covers off, I jumped out of bed and marched my horny ass out of the room in search of my missing roommate.

Finding him didn't take long. He stood in the kitchen, shirtless despite the winter chill in the air. A winter chill that wouldn't exist if he would let me turn the heat up to at least seventy-five, I might add. His novelty Christmas sleep pants with the gamer reindeer hung low on his hips, showing off his delicious V and my favorite tattoos, the NES blasters.

I stood just outside the kitchen, licking my lips as I watched him, waiting for him to acknowledge me instead of the phone attached to his ear.

"She's up now, Fran. I'll be sure to ask her once I'm off the phone," he said without even glancing my way.

I rolled my eyes. Of course he was talking to my mom. He kept in contact with her more than any of her biological kids. It was strange considering he hadn't spoken to his own parents since before we met. Or maybe that was why he latched onto my mom.

I didn't know the story behind his life before me. Anytime I asked, he found a way to change the subject or distract me. Jack wasn't much help, either. The most I knew was that they both attended a fancy academy pre-k through high school. I thought that might mean they were both loaded, but that theory went out the window when I met Jack's family at his and Sophie's wedding. They were as blue collar as they came. What I did learn was the academy had a very generous scholarship program for lower income households.

Eventually, I gave up trying to figure it out. There was probably some trauma involved, and as much as it hurt that Nixon didn't want to share, I knew I needed to respect that. Not everyone found healing in trauma dumping the way I did.

"Yes, we got the packages in the mail earlier this week...I told Poppy to text you that they arrived...Yes, I saw the ones labeled for Christmas Eve...We actually have a full day today. They might not get opened until late, but we'll make sure to at least text you pictures," Nixon continued.

I let out a long, overexaggerated sigh, signaling my displeasure at being ignored before closing in on my prey.

Nixon turned to watch me, still talking on the phone, as I drew closer. He raised an eyebrow in question when I stopped directly in front of him. The curious expression morphed to panic as I dropped to my knees.

What are you doing? he silently mouthed.

I answered by pulling down his pants and boxers in one swift tug. There might have been fear in his eyes, but his already stiff cock told another story. It stood proud and definitely excited for what was to come.

"Um, yes. I'm still here," Nixon said, his voice cracking under the pressure as his eyes continued to watch with a mix of horror and anticipation.

A better friend would have backed down, but not me. I took a special glee in forcing Nixon to surrender to pleasure at the most inappropriate moments, and no time was more inappropriate than now.

I placed one hand on his hip for support, wrapping the other around the base of his shaft. I could feel his heated gaze watching as I leaned closer, inspecting the silver piercings that decorated his dick. Taking my time, I flicked the apadravya piercing with my tongue, relishing the strain in Nixon's voice as he tried to continue the phone conversation like nothing was wrong.

Pushing things further, I wrapped my lips around his cock and sucked hard. Nixon's eyes fell shut as his free hand reached down and fisted my hair, holding me in place. When he opened his beautiful brown eyes, there was a dark hunger glowing in them that wasn't there before.

"Fran, I'm going to let you go," he said between shallow thrusts. "Yeah, your daughter's being a bit of a brat...No, no. I can handle her just fine on my own...Yeah...Merry Christmas to you, too."

He tossed the phone on the kitchen counter as a string of colorful curses fell from his lips. Without any distractions, his whole aura shifted to one of both dominance and desperation as he began thrusting harder into my mouth.

"That was fucked up, even for you, Pops," he scolded, his hips picking up speed. "You wake up that hungry for my cock?"

I smiled around his hard length, drool spilling from my mouth. It wasn't cock specifically that I wanted, any orgasms would do. Though I wasn't going to come if I stayed on my knees the whole time.

Satisfied that I now had Nixon's undivided attention, I tried to stand. His grip tightened, holding me in place, as he chuckled between moans.

"I don't think so, Pops. You're going to finish what you started," he said, thrusting deeper.

Ha. Ha. Ha. No. Did Nixon forget who he was dealing with?

The quickest way to get me to do something was to try to force me to do the opposite. Maybe if Nixon praised my efforts and begged me not to stop, I might have seen it through. Instead, he tried to assert control when I was already in a bratty mood.

You brought this on yourself, I thought as I pinched his hip and twisted hard. Nixon yelped, releasing me as he jumped back.

"What the fuck?" he exclaimed, rubbing the sore spot.

His face scrunched into a frown as he flashed me a look of betrayal. *Whatever.* I rolled my eyes, unimpressed with his dramatics. If he hadn't wanted me to attack, he should have behaved.

"It's your fault for not letting me stand," I said as I got to my feet. Nixon huffed.

"Three taps is our signal when you can't speak," he reminded me.

I stared at him, blinking in disbelief. Was he really scolding me right now?

It was a struggle to take the conversation seriously with Nixon in a state of undress in the middle of the kitchen. Especially since my needs hadn't been met. Honestly, it was borderline rude of the man to keep taunting me with his dick. He should have been trying to coax me into the bedroom, promising sweet orgasms if I finished the job. Instead, he wanted to argue.

"But it wasn't that kind of situation. I just wanted to stop on principle," I explained.

Maybe he was right, maybe I should have tapped out, but I hated using any sort of safe signal if there wasn't a valid reason. I wasn't in pain or panicked. I just wanted to stand. Why would I use a distress signal for that?

"Principle? You are such an ass sometimes. Why even drop to your knees if you don't plan to follow through?" he grumbled.

That was a fair point, but I was in a mood—a playful, bratty mood, to be exact. Unfortunately, my actions had not translated the way I had intended and now I had a pouting Nixon.

Ugh!

None of this was going the way I wanted, not that I should be surprised. Acting out was never useful in getting what I wanted out of Nixon. Unlike certain exes who saw my brattiness as a challenge, being bratty with Nixon usually caused a fight.

I sighed, looking around the kitchen as I tried to figure out how to salvage the morning. It was Christmas Eve—a time of magic, food, friends, and fucking. Well, maybe not fucking, but my horny little brain couldn't get my naked roommate out of my head.

My thoughts halted as I turned toward the counter and finally noticed the lone plate sitting there—a poached egg sitting on top of smoked salmon and an English muffin, with hollandaise sauce drizzled on top.

"What's this?" I asked, turning back to Nixon.

He held my eyes as he stepped forward, still without clothes.

"Um, your breakfast? I woke up early to surprise you," he replied.

He woke up early to surprise me with breakfast. That was such a Nixon thing to do. And what did I do? Gave the man blue balls for not licking my pussy.

"Why is there only one?" I asked, trying not to look down at the erection pointing at me. *Focus, Poppy. No dick for you...yet.*

Nixon shrugged. "Because I don't like Eggs Benedict. I was planning on popping a frozen waffle in the toaster for me."

All the playfulness drained right out of me, guilt taking its place. As far as I knew, Nixon had never poached an egg before. It was something he probably learned on the fly this morning. For me.

"Why do you have to be so damn thoughtful," I grumbled.

A soft laugh escaped him as he wrapped his arms around my waist, pulling my body to his. The atmosphere between us instantly shifted from adversarial to something more intimate and calm as I melted against him.

"I'm not going to apologize for doing nice things for you. I like taking care of you," he breathed.

His arms tightened around me like I was a precious treasure he thought he might lose. The moment was pure, aside from the steel rod poking me, reminding me my roomie was both naked and aroused. But that was us, and why we worked.

"I'm sorry," I whispered as I nuzzled into his warm body.

"What's that? I didn't quite hear you. Did you say you're sorry?" he taunted.

Asshole.

Letting out a frustrated growl, I tried to pull away, but Nixon only tightened his hold on me.

"Woah, hey. Sorry, sorry. I know that was hard for you," he said, trying to calm me down.

"Whatever, jerk," I muttered before leaning down and biting his nipple.

Nixon hissed and then groaned as his hips thrust involuntarily. My Nixy loved a little pain with his pleasure, though not nearly as much as I did.

"Don't tease unless you plan to follow through," he warned. The dark hunger in his voice was absolutely delicious, and it reminded me why I came out here looking for him in the first place.

"Let me ride your face until I come, Nixy."

Chapter 2
Breakfast Between Thighs

Nixon

When your best friend said she wanted to ride your face, the only correct response was to say fuck yeah. Without hesitation, I scooped Poppy into my arms and carried her to my bedroom, leaving my discarded clothes in the kitchen. I wouldn't need them for what I had planned. Her melodic laughter echoed through our rented home as her arms tightened around my neck. The absolute joy that radiated from her as she clung to me was infectious.

"Eager much?" she teased with a giggle.

"To taste that sweet pussy? Always," I replied.

I knew I was staring back at her with the goofiest grin on my face, but I couldn't help it. There was something about diving face first between Poppy's thighs that made me feel like the luckiest man alive. My cock was hard as a rock just thinking about it.

Opening the door with full arms was a less than graceful feat. Poppy giggling at my struggles didn't help either, but I was determined. First, I was going to lick her cunt until my face was dripping with her juices, then I was going to relieve my own building frustrations.

Once inside, I gently laid my best friend on my bed like the precious cargo she was. She looked stunning stretched out on my Spider-Man sheets, even if she was fully covered by her tacky Krampus pj's. I couldn't help but take a moment to soak in the vision that she was.

Her hooded gaze dropped to my hand, watching me slowly stroke myself as I admired her. Those perfect lips parted just enough for her tongue to peek out and slide over the top. She was the embodiment of sex, even in her goofy pajamas.

"I can't ride your face with you all the way over there," she said, patting the space next to her on the bed.

Pouncing, I leaned down and bit Poppy's hip through her clothing. She gave a little squeal and squirmed, but I didn't let her get away.

With a smile on my lips, I began the task of undressing the object of my desires. I was a kid on Christmas, unwrapping the giant box under the tree. *Only this box is much tighter.*

Poppy gave me a curious look as I chuckled at my pun. I shook it off, pretending I didn't notice as I tossed her sleepwear off the bed. As amusing as my joke was to me, I doubt she would be impressed, and I really didn't want to ruin the mood. Too much was at stake.

Naked and beautiful, Poppy raised her arms above her head and gave a long stretch. The way her body arched, pointing her tits upward, made my cock weep with joy. She was a piece of fucking art.

I took one of those beautiful breasts into my mouth and groaned in satisfaction as I sucked her nipple until it hardened. Poppy's fingers tangled in my hair as she held me in place, a soft moan falling from her lips. This was heaven, my very own happily ever after.

Except it wasn't really the ever after of our story. This was merely an interlude between relationships. At the stroke of midnight on New Year's Eve, our little pact would pull a Cinderella and we'd go back to the way things were before—friends. Yes, we'd still fuck, but there was so much more to a relationship than sex.

The last few weeks had been everything I ever dreamed of and more. I asked Poppy for the whole package, and she delivered. She had cut back exponentially on flirting with other people, initiated PDA frequently, and the cuddles lately were next level. The thought of giving all of that up was more upsetting than I wanted to admit.

Focus on the task at hand. If you do a good job, she'll be begging to make it permanent. That thought perked me right up.

With renewed excitement, I bit Poppy's nipple hard enough to elicit a cute little squeak. Then, I moved to the other breast, repeating the action.

With my hands on her hips, I held Poppy in place while I continued to tease her luscious tits until she was a squirming, whining mess underneath me. I wanted her to need me as much as I needed her. I wanted her pushed so far over the edge she could no longer think.

I let one of my hands travel downward. The tips of my fingers ghosted over her clit with the lightest of touches. Poppy's hips bucked in search of more friction as a feral whine left her lips.

"Stop teasing motherfucker, or—"

"Or what?" I asked between nipping at the sides of her breasts. "You'll go to your room and finish yourself?"

Poppy growled as I circled her soaking wet entrance, still denying her anything more. Her whole body was taut with frustration, her grip on my hair tight enough to cause pain, but I ignored it all. She was so close to breaking.

"We both know that won't happen." I continued to taunt her while I touched her everywhere but where she wanted. "If you were going to do that, you wouldn't have come out to the kitchen. No, you want me to be the one to get you off. You want it so bad, don't you?"

"Yes." The word was so faint that I almost missed it.

"Hm? Did you say something, Pops?"

I slipped the tip of my finger just barely inside her before pulling back out. The anguished cry that escaped her made my cock throb. It was rare that Poppy would let me tease her for any real amount of time without restraints. She usually grew impatient and took over, but now she was pliant and ready to beg.

"Please, Nixon."

And there it was, the two sweetest words in existence.

I rewarded Poppy by sinking my finger a little deeper inside her while biting her nipple. Then I pulled out, sliding my finger upward between her slick folds.

Her reaction—a momentary burst of relief instantly replaced with more frustration—was beautiful. It filled me with a sense of power that drove me to test her limits.

"I think you can beg a little better than that, Poppy. How badly do you want it?" I continued to taunt her as my fingers skillfully teased her pussy.

She was a dripping mess, and we'd only just begun. Poppy wasn't alone. I was hanging on by a thread myself. The only thing holding me back was my need to watch her shatter under my touch.

"So bad. Fuck! Please, Nixon! Please! I'll do anything you want. Anything! I fucking swear, just please!" she begged in desperation.

Tears fell from her eyes as she continued to beg, promising me anything and everything under the sun. Her pain was delicious. It was a need so great that she couldn't survive without relief. A relief only I could provide.

"Anything?" I finally asked, cutting her rambling pleas short.

"Yes," she choked out as her hips continued to chase my touch, which was just out of reach.

"Free use for the rest of the day. Whatever I want, whenever I want—no pushback," I started.

I added the last bit because I knew Poppy all too well. I might have had her pliant now, but those moments were few and far between. Once the post orgasms bliss faded, she'd be back to the mouthy little brat who loved to take control. I didn't want that today. I wanted the good girl, desperate to please me however I wish.

Poppy nodded as she whimpered in frustration.

"That's not good enough, Pops. I need to hear you say it," I said with a deep, husky voice.

I learned my lesson years ago. If I didn't hear her say it, I couldn't be sure she knew what she was agreeing to. Once she even tried to claim after that she wasn't nodding, she was wiggling with pleasure. *Yeah, right.*

"Free use the rest of the day. Anything you want, it's yours. Just tongue my pussy already!" she snapped.

I chuckled, a smug grin tugging at my lips. I *won*.

"As you wish," I said with dark joy.

I wanted to taste her, but there were other things I wanted, too. Now I had the permission I needed to fulfill my every fantasy.

Poppy let out a frustrated growl as I pulled away to reposition myself. *Impatient as ever.*

"Calm down, woman! You can't ride me if you're the one on your back," I snapped.

Poppy scooted over, giving me ample space to lie flat. Then she leaned forward, carefully removing my glasses. I watched with slightly blurred vision as she placed them on the nightstand next to my bed before turning her attention back to me, watching me position myself.

Poppy was beautiful, towering over me in all of her naked glory. I didn't need twenty-twenty vision to see that. Watching the way her body twisted and turned as she straddled my face made my dick ache with need.

Without a conscious thought, I grabbed my throbbing cock and gave it a few leisurely strokes, my eyes never leaving the perfect pussy that hovered above me. This wasn't where I expected to be Christmas Eve morning, but I wasn't going to complain.

After a few seconds of hesitation, Poppy lowered herself so her cunt was flush with my face. I groaned in satisfaction from my first lick. Pussy was pussy—it all tasted the same, but there was just something about Poppy's that drove me fucking wild.

"Oh, fuck." The small curse flowed into a soft moan as Poppy rocked her hips.

Focusing solely on her pleasure, I released my hold on my cock so I could grip Poppy's ass with both hands. My fingers dug in, holding her firmly in place so I could work my magic.

I don't know how long I was under her, not that it mattered. Time was meaningless. Yes, we had plans, but they were inconsequential compared to the heavenly bliss that was Poppy riding my face like she owned it. My tongue swirled inside her, teasing her as I hummed over her swollen sex. Her cursing became louder and more erratic as she closed in on the finish line.

Changing tactics, I focused on her clit, swirling my tongue around the sensitive little bud until I felt her body seize above me. Pride washed over me as she shrieked in unholy pleasure. I knew the sound well—Poppy was coming hard.

The moment her orgasm finished, her whole body went limp. I awkwardly helped her off me, enjoying how fuck-drunk she looked with hooded eyes and a dazed expression. *I did that.*

"Merry Christmas to me," she mumbled, barely coherent.

I laughed as I rolled off the bed and gathered her clothes from around my room.

"Enjoy yourself?" I teased.

She smiled for a second, but it quickly faded when I handed Poppy her clothes.

"Don't you want me to take care of that?" she asked, motioning to my erection.

"Soon enough," I replied, "but I don't want your breakfast to go to waste."

Poppy gave me a look that said she wasn't convinced, but she didn't argue.

The truth was, I was dying for my own sweet relief, but I wasn't lying about her breakfast. I went to great lengths to get everything without Poppy catching on so I could surprise her. I could wait a little longer, especially since I now had a free pass to do whatever I wanted with her body for the rest of the day. There would be plenty of orgasms in my future. I just had to be patient.

Chapter 3
Christmas Kittens

Poppy

*C*ookies—check. Christmas cake—check. Gift baskets for every-one—check. Prep for tomorrow's Christmas brunch—check.

I mentally ran through the list of everything I needed to do before we headed over to Jack and Sophie's place for their annual Christmas Eve luncheon. For once, I was running right on schedule.

Their event wasn't a potluck like my Friendsgiving celebration. They provided a few different charcuterie boards and some hearty appetizers that were more than filling, but neither was super into baking, so they always outsourced that part. I didn't mind one bit. I loved baking sweets and trying new recipes.

This year, I experimented with a hot cocoa cookie recipe that came out divine after the third tweak. The first batch wasn't even bad. I just felt my taste testers, AKA my coworkers, weren't enthusiastic enough with their praise. Third time's a charm, and even

I couldn't deny what a great job I did. *And hopefully batch four turned out the same.*

Covering tomorrow's French toast casserole with foil, I then took the strawberry Christmas cake out of the fridge, moving the casserole in its place. *Perfect.*

"Really? No Christmas sweater?" Nixon remarked.

I turned to find him standing in the entryway of the kitchen, staring at me with a look of disappointment.

"What?" I said, looking down at my outfit. "You don't like it?"

I had put a lot of thought and effort into my current ensemble. The high-waisted, pleated skirt in Christmas tartan was a thrift find that I bought and tailored, raising the hem so it fell about a hand's length past my ass. *Short, but not too short.* The black sweater was admittedly not one of the many novelty Christmas sweaters I owned, but it matched the black, textured thigh-high stockings I wore. I tied the whole thing together with a sinfully red no smudge lipstick and matching Mary Jane wedges.

Nixon's eyes raked over my body, slowly drinking me in. The frown never left his lips, but the dark hunger clouding his eyes said he wasn't as upset as he wanted me to think.

"You look beautiful. But..." His words drifted as he looked down at his own Christmas sweater.

It wasn't your average full-coverage sweater that most ugly Christmas sweaters were. No, his was a v-neck that let his red, collared shirt and green bowtie peak out. The sweater itself was decorated with little kittens wearing their Christmas finest—something I had gotten for him our third Christmas together.

It was clear by the way he was staring at his own outfit that he felt lacking in some way. The notion was ridiculous, of course. Nixon looked like sex on a stick, even with the Christmas kittens.

It's the skinny jeans, I told myself. Anytime he paired a button down, collared shirt and bowtie with skinny jeans, my panties melted. The combination with his black-framed glasses really sold the whole sexy hipster vibe.

Unfortunately, my bestie wasn't feeling the confident panty melter that he was at the moment. That wouldn't do at all.

I walked over, reaching out to trace the little kittens with my fingers. They were fluff balls of faux fur, still soft to the touch after all these years.

"But what? I love your kitten sweater. It's one of my favorites," I cooed.

Nixon looked up, his expression silently saying "They're all your favorites."

It's true. I loved this time of year with all the celebrations and traditions, even the ones rooted in evil capitalism. For me, the holidays were about family, friendship, and making someone's day brighter.

"Whatever. I picked this out thinking you were going to wear one of yours. Now I just feel silly," he pouted.

"I've actually worn all of mine at least once," I stated.

That wasn't completely true. There was one I hadn't worn yet, but that was because it was strictly for Christmas day. Either way, it didn't matter. Nixon's issue wasn't actually with what I wore. He didn't want to stick out.

"You know others will be dressed up in way goofier sweaters than yours," I continued, trying to appease him.

Nixon folded his arms as he rolled his head side to side, mulling over my words. Any other day I would have told him to go change, but I loved him in that sweater.

"I guess," he finally conceded, then adding, "and you do look very nice."

"I know, right?" I said with the biggest grin.

Taking a few steps backward, I did a little twirl as a giggle broke free. That's all it took to make Nixon's sour expression melt away. He took the few steps needed to close the gap between us, wrapping an arm around my waist, effectively trapping my body against his. His free hand dropped to my thigh, his fingers tracing the lace patterns of my stockings.

"I love you, Pops. You know that, right?" he said with a sincerity I had never heard before.

With most anyone else, those words would have carried an uncomfortable weight. Nixon was different—special. He was family, the other piece of my soul, my best friend. That's why we worked so well, even when we were with other people. When you truly love someone, you only want their happiness.

"Of course you do. What's not to love?" I teased, trying to lighten the atmosphere.

"What, indeed," he agreed.

His lips quirked upward into a gentle smile as he leaned down, resting his forehead on mine. The move felt intimate, far more intimate than a simple holiday pact. It hadn't gone unnoticed that this sort of behavior was happening more frequently. Nixon seemed determined to push the boundaries of our pact, blurring the lines we'd been so careful to preserve.

I tried to pull back, but Nixon tightened his hold as his fingers trailed higher. He sucked in a breath when he ventured under my skirt and found where my stockings ended. My Nixy was a sucker for thigh-highs.

Goosebumps rose along my bare skin, trailing behind his fingers as they climbed higher.

"You're trying to drive me crazy, aren't you?" he said breathlessly.

"Maybe." *Yes.*

I planned the outfit weeks in advance with the sole purpose of driving Nixon wild, but he didn't need to know that.

I didn't keep many secrets, but the ones I had were pretty big—like how I unknowingly dated the CFO of the company we work for before Nixon got me a position there (*and occasionally picked up where we left off whenever Nixon was in a relationship and I wasn't*). And while planning an outfit to drive my BFF wild might not seem like it was on the same level, to me it was. It was basically admitting I thought about him more than I should.

It wasn't that I feared rejection. It was the opposite, actually. Nixon would want to plow ahead full steam with all of his stupid romantic ideals only to be let down when the reality didn't match up to everything he built up in his head. He was such an overly romantic dreamer who wore his heart on his sleeve, even if he swore the opposite. I'd seen what happened when he fell head over heels, throwing his everything into a relationship. And I had been there to pick up the pieces after everything crashed and burned. Hell, that's how we ended up roommates in the first place.

We had a good thing going, and as much as it hurt sometimes to think about what could be if I gave us a real chance, the pain was better than losing the one person who ever truly saw me for me.

With that in mind, I changed tactics. Tilting my head upward, I grabbed Nixon's lower lip between my teeth and gave a soft tug. With hooded eyes, he let out a groan that rolled into a hungry growl. The primal sound made my pussy wet and my nipples hardened.

I sucked in a breath, caught off guard by how much my body was reacting to his response. Nixon chased after my lips as soon as I released him, kissing me with a passion I rarely experienced. My panties melted as his tongue expertly dismantled my defenses and shut down my brain. All that existed was Nixon, me, and this fiery passion that engulfed our very beings. By the time Nixon pulled back, I was a panting mess unable to form a coherent thought.

He released me from his hold, taking a step back so his eyes could rake over my body once more. I stood there like an idiot, barely able to stand after what he had just done.

It was just a kiss, I chided myself. *You've been kissed hundreds of times!* Yes, but I've never been kissed like that before. Not by Nixon. Not by anyone.

"What do you have for me under that skirt, Poppy?" It wasn't a question. It was an order.

His aura radiated power as he stared me down while palming his cock. A shiver of excitement ran down my spine as my fingers reached for the hem of my skirt. Nixon's eyes immediately dropped down, following my hands as they slowly lifted the fabric. He let out another groan, his knees almost buckling underneath him, when I exposed my red lace thong with holly embroidered on the front.

"Fuck, woman! How am I supposed to function today knowing *that's* what you've got going on under your skirt?"

He dropped to his knees in front of me, pulling me closer. His fingers dug into my fleshy ass as he buried his face into my crotch, nuzzling against the fabric. I reached out and grabbed his shoulders for support, trying to stay on my feet.

Closing my eyes, I focused on the sparks of pleasure that danced over my skin as Nixon nipped and licked my mound through the lace. Then a finger joined the mix, slipping under the fabric and pushing inside. A soft *fuck* fell from my lips, followed by a moan as my hips rocked in response.

It all felt so good, aside from the strain in my legs to keep myself upright. Nixon pumped a single finger inside of me while the warmth of his tongue teased me through my thong. My finger dug into his shoulders until my knuckles were sore as I rode the wave of pleasure. A second finger was added, the sweet burn stretching in the best way.

This wasn't our first time fucking around in the kitchen—there wasn't a surface in our home that we hadn't christened—but we'd never done anything quite like this, standing in the middle of a room. At the moment, I didn't exactly care, aside from the pain in my knees and thighs from trying not to topple over. As nice as it would have been to sit, or even lie on the floor, I didn't want to stop and risk breaking the magic.

I was close, so damn close. Nixon was humming with delight as he worked my body. His sounds of contentment blended with the colorful curses that fell from my lips, filling the room around us. I was barely aware of the sounds we were making until a high-pitched whine burst from me. Nixon knew what that meant, and nipped at my clit, sending me over the edge.

My muscles locked in place as the orgasm coursed through me—wave after wave of pleasure. It wasn't the Earth shattering O I had only a few hours prior, but it left me sated and limp, nonetheless.

Nixon pulled back, staring up at me from the ground with a smug expression.

"Proud of yourself?" I teased.

"I made a beautiful woman come twice in one morning when most men go their entire lives without accomplishing such a feat even once," he replied.

Chapter 4
Sweet Release

Nixon

Poppy scoffed at my little comment and rolled her eyes, clearly unimpressed. *Whatever.* I knew just how impressive it was to get her off.

We'd been best friends for years, making me privy to a lot of information—like how many guys could get her over the finish line. Spoiler alert, not many.

Poppy thought she had commitment issues, but really it was a lack of patience. If a guy couldn't rock her socks by the second time in bed, she wasn't going to stick around for a third. She wanted instant gratification and a mind reader.

The only reason I succeeded where many had failed was because I insisted on a lot of communication early on in our situationship. When you come out of a breakup that took you by surprise, you want a lot of reassurance that you are doing the right thing. All that communication gave me the tools and knowledge I needed to satisfy my best friend. Every. Single. Time.

"Help me up?" I asked, reaching toward her.

Poppy grabbed my hand, taking a few steps backward to help pull me to my feet. Once I was standing, her eyes dropped to the very noticeable bulge in my pants. I tried to adjust myself, but there was no hiding my erection in skinny jeans.

"Maybe you should wear looser pants," Poppy said with a smirk.

Closing the distance between us, I grabbed her by the waist and spun her around so her back was flush against my chest. My cock throbbed with longing, eager to plunge inside her.

Leaning down, I nipped at her neck, savoring the little yelps that escaped as she squirmed in my hold.

"Or maybe I should bend you over and fuck that dripping pussy until it's full of my cum," I whispered against the shell of her ear.

Poppy shivered as she moaned, pushing her ass into me. *Fuck.* She wanted it bad. I wanted her, too, but not so bad that I was willing to risk injuring her.

Guiding her to the kitchen island, I pressed down between her shoulder blades, forcing her to bend over the counter. She didn't resist, her body moving fluidly into position as I arranged her.

She was being such a good girl, and it was driving me fucking wild. My cock ached to sink into her and feel her tight warmth strangle me.

Patience, the little voice reminded me. I sucked in a sharp breath, forcing myself to remain in control. Poppy may have been dripping wet, but she still needed to be stretched.

Keeping my left hand splayed across her back, I reached down with my right hand, slipping two fingers past her thong. I groaned as her wet heat tightened around my digits, showing me just how hungry her cunt was for my cock. Fuck, she was perfect.

Starting slow, I thrusted my fingers in and out, savoring the way she squirmed and whimpered under my attention. Poppy was already so wet that the movement created the lewdest noises as I worked her body.

Gradually, I picked up the pace, adding another finger for good measure. The way she moaned in response made my cock throb. I wanted to be in her so damn bad, but I didn't want to stop the show.

Pleasuring Poppy was one of my favorite hobbies. It was an ego thing. I loved being the source of my partner's pleasure, and it didn't matter whether I was the one in control or them. Poppy and I had been on and off physically since the second week I crashed on her couch all those years ago. We had intimate knowledge of each other, the kind of knowledge that made me feel like a god when I played with her.

Poppy's fingers scratched at the counter surface as a mangled squeal of pleasure echoed through the kitchen. Her dripping pussy contracted around my fingers—yet another orgasm ripping through her—signaling she was finally ready.

Removing my slick fingers, I worked quickly to free my dick from its overly tight confinement. I gave myself a few leisurely pumps as I marveled at the panting, sated beauty bent over in front of me. I did that... and I was about to do more.

Lifting her skirt, I pulled the thong to the side and lined myself up with her entrance. Then, with both hands on her hips, I pressed in at an agonizingly slow pace. Poppy made the most beautiful whimpers as I filled her, inch by inch. It was heavenly torture, taking my time when all I wanted to do was let loose.

All the way in, I took a moment to recenter myself. I'd been teetering on the edge since her beautiful lips were wrapped around my cock earlier in the morning. The last thing I needed was to blow my load on the second thrust. No, I wanted to enjoy myself.

"You've already come more than enough this morning. Now it's time for you to be a good little fuck doll," I rasped, barely able to speak.

Poppy made a sound of agreement that was more a moan than anything as she clenched her walls around me. *Fuck.*

I took my palm to her ass and gave it a smack, enjoying the way she screamed out another moan.

"Be a good girl and use your words. Who's my little fuck doll?" I demanded softly.

"I—I am." Her voice quivered as she struggled to say two little words.

"Damn fucking straight," I said as I gave her ass another smack.

Confident I had my shit under control, I started to move, slowly pulling out before easing myself back in. Whispered curses fell from my lips as I realized just how far from in control I really was.

Everything felt good—too good. Her cunt squeezed me like a heavenly vise, my piercings adding extra spikes of pleasure as they rubbed against her walls. I was overwhelmed by all of it, unable to think past my primal need for more.

The sounds of slapping skin mixed with a wet squelching noise as my hips picked up the pace. Poppy egged me on, randomly shouting "Harder." "Faster." "More." It was all a blur, fading into pleasure as I pistoned into her dripping cunt.

It was like I was in some sort of porn—girl bent over in the kitchen, acting like she actually enjoyed getting jack hammered. The whole thing was ridiculous, but it made it so much hotter somehow.

It wasn't until after my orgasm came crashing over me—my whole body shaking from overstimulation—that my mind cleared enough to realize how rough I had been. All the pleasure in the world didn't matter if it injured her in the process.

I stilled, catching my breath as I tried to gauge if she was okay.

"I know that wasn't about me, but—fuck—that was amazing, Nixy," Poppy said between heavy breaths.

Her praise was enough to ease my conscience. If she enjoyed it, then everything was okay...even if she was fighting back a wince as she stood upright and adjusted herself.

Without saying a word, Poppy slipped her hand into mine. The gesture surprised me, but I wasn't about to look a gift horse in the mouth. Interlacing our fingers, I tried to pull her into a hug, but she only let me tug her so close.

"Woah, buddy. You still got your dick out, and it's covered in sex juices. I don't need that on the front of my skirt," she said.

"Sex juices?" I repeated, arching a brow.

"Yes, sex juices. Now, come on. I need to clean the jizz off and change panties before we leave. Thankfully, I have another thong for the occasion," Poppy said with faux annoyance.

She could pretend she was upset over the panties, but the blissed-out look in her eyes gave her away.

"Or, you could skip panties all together," I offered.

Poppy scoffed as she tugged me along.

Chapter 5
Real Friends

Nixon

I hate Christmas music with a passion. Blame my brief stint working retail after I got kicked out of my home. College was no longer an option—and I needed money if I didn't want to leech off Jack's family indefinitely—so I took a job at the first place that would hire me.

Retail work during the holidays was bad enough—crankier than usual customers, extended store hours, influx of seasonal hires that had no idea what they were doing—but the music sent me over the edge.

The store I worked at had a playlist of about forty songs, which doesn't sound bad in theory, but that's only two and a half hours of music. Music that's replayed over and over and over for almost a month. There was no break, no new song slipped in, just the same two and a half hours looping over your eight-hour shift, five days a week.

I couldn't even escape the torture when I left since the songs were generic enough that every other store—and even some radio stations—played them. It was hell on earth.

Unfortunately for me, I was madly in love with a woman who loved Christmas music. Over the course of her lifetime, Poppy had amassed quite the collection. The vast majority of her collection was MP3s that she kept several backups of between cloud storage and thumb drives, but she still had a few CDs tucked away for emergencies.

Immersing herself in the music was part of the holiday experience for Poppy. Her smile lit up brighter than a Christmas tree whenever her playlist was on full blast. It didn't matter the genre, as long as it was about the holiday season it was enough.

And that's why I currently sat in the front passenger seat with a tight smile on my face, praying for death, as she belted out the words to Lady Gaga's "Christmas Tree" while the song blared through the car speakers. *Dear God, kill me now.*

"Could we turn the music down a little, at least?" I asked when the song ended.

Poppy gave a playful huff as she rolled her eyes with faux annoyance. She knew I hated the music, and she knew the reason, but it didn't deter her.

"I guess, *Scrooge*," she teased as she reached out and adjusted the volume.

"Scrooge? Really? Do you not see my kittens?" I motioned to my sweater. "Would a Scrooge wear a sweater adorned with over-the-top Christmas kittens?"

That earned me a weird little snort-laugh that made me smile. She briefly glanced my way, giving me a wink before returning her attention to the road.

"For the record, you look hot in that sweater," Poppy said, as if she was the undisputed authority on the matter.

I scoffed. "Yeah, okay."

There was nothing hot about my Christmas sweater. The only reason I still had it was because of who gave it to me. Most of my holiday sweaters were from Poppy, and she always noticed if I skipped wearing any. I didn't usually mind indulging since she'd be wearing an equally tacky sweater, but today was different. She looked fucking amazing while I was wearing cats.

"No, I'm serious. And it's definitely a conversation starter. I'm going to have to keep my eyes on you during the pub crawl," she insisted.

I turned to face Poppy, taking a moment to study her expression. She was all business with her eyes straight ahead, not a hint of her usual playfulness. *Interesting.*

"What? Are you jealous? Worried a couple of hypothetical Christmas cuties might steal me away?" I teased.

Poppy rolled her eyes as she shook her head.

"No one could steal you from me," she stated confidently, then adding, "But that sweater is definitely Christmas cutie catnip."

I groaned at the terrible pun as she burst into a fit of laughter. Despite my outward cringing, I was absolutely beaming on the inside. While she was doing a good job of hiding it, I knew Poppy well enough to know she wasn't entirely joking. There was genuine concern laced in her teasing words. *Poppy's jealous.*

***

The driveway was already filled by the time we arrived at Jack and Sophie's, leaving us to park by the curb. Poppy let out a little huff to remind me she hated parking on the street. You would have thought we were parked three blocks over by the sour look on her face.

"This is actually a blessing in disguise," I said as I opened the passenger door. "Now you don't have to worry about being blocked in when we're ready to leave."

An adorable little grunt was her only response as she got out of the car and grabbed the desserts, leaving me to unload all the gifts we brought. I looked at the box bursting at the seams with colorful gift bags and let out a small sigh before grabbing them.

Inside, the festivities were in full swing. People gathered in small groups, indulging in the hors d'oeuvres Jack and Sophie provided. Their conversations were a low hum, barely drowning out the soft jazz playing through the speakers over the crackling fireplace.

I moved through the crowd, nodding brief hellos as I made my way to the kitchen where Poppy was already in full conversation with Sophie.

"Merry Christmas!" Sophie greeted me excitedly as she tried to hug me. Unfortunately, the cumbersome box made it more than a little difficult.

"Merry Christmas, Soph. I'd hug you back but—" I lifted the box slightly.

"Drop the box in the guest room. I'll divvy up the gifts after I get the desserts out," Poppy instructed with a wave of her hand.

I wanted to make a snappy remark about making me do the heavy lifting, but decided it was better to hold my tongue. I didn't want to risk Poppy misunderstanding and end up in a fight over a box that I wouldn't have let her carry on her own, anyway.

Moving back through the crowd, I headed toward the guest room. It was a small room that barely fit the queen bed inside it. A twin would have made much more sense, but the room was used most often by Poppy and me after one too many drinks. A twin wasn't going to fit both of us, and one of us sleeping on the couch always led to bickering. The fact that Jack and Sophie purchased an extra queen bed for Poppy and me said all it needed to about our friendship with the couple.

Setting the box down on the bed, I gave my arms a long stretch to try to relieve some of the tension.

"Knock, knock," Jack called from the doorway, lightly tapping on the open door.

I turned to see him leaning on the doorframe, one arm hidden behind his back.

"Hey! Merry Christmas," I greeted.

Jack took a step forward, arm still behind his back. *Not suspicious at all.*

"Merry Christmas, man. I wanted to catch you before you started mingling," he said as he entered the room.

I couldn't help noticing the way he hid one hand behind his back as he walked toward me with a smile on his face. I loved Jack, but he wasn't the best at subtly.

"Yeah? Everything okay?" I asked.

Instead of answering, he thrust a small, colorfully wrapped package into my hands. I looked down at the present as I accepted it before looking back up at Jack.

"Um, thanks," I said cautiously.

My curiosity piqued, I took a moment to inspect the present, trying to guess what was inside. It was no bigger than a notebook, and just as thin. No, thinner. *Definitely not an action figure*, I thought to myself. The box was too long to be a gift card, but not much else made sense.

The wrapping paper was blue with little Spider-Man heads wearing Santa hats tiling across. Was that a clue or did he merely pick out the paper because of my obsession with the web slinger?

I looked back at Jack, who was watching me with anticipation. I raised a brow, silently asking for a clue. He shook his head before nodding toward the gift, urging me to open it already. The man was practically giddy with excitement.

Without a word, I carefully unwrapped the mystery gift, unsure what was waiting beneath the paper. The fact that Jack got me a gift at all was something. Normally, it was Sophie who did the gifting for the both of them.

Wrapping paper on the floor, I opened the thin, brown box, my hands shaking when I saw what was inside.

"Amazing Spider-Man number seventeen? This—this is an original," I said, looking up at Jack in disbelief.

"It's your original, actually," he replied.

My original? No, that wasn't possible. My copy—

"I—I don't understand," I whispered as I tried to hold back tears. So many emotions I repressed for so long were on the verge of bursting out of me.

While my parents indulged in most of my whims growing up, comics were the one exception. If it wasn't something flashy that advertised their wealth, they weren't interested.

My grandparents, may they rest in peace, were a different story. They didn't have the same need as my parents to flaunt their wealth. In fact, they preferred to be more subtle about things. Their gifts were by no means cheap, but they had significantly more thought put into them—like when my grandfather gifted me an original Spider-Man number seventeen for my fourteenth birthday.

When my parents kicked me out, it was pretty instant. They barred me from getting any of my things. Jack was able to get inside and grab a handful of my belongings, though he never exactly explained how. Most of the items weren't anything of crazy value, just a few odd and ends from my childhood. And while I was grateful for what he was able to recover, I couldn't deny the sense of loss I felt for certain items.

"I didn't want to tell you at the time because you were dealing with so much, but I tracked where your parents sold and donated a lot of your stuff after kicking you out. The comic was sold to a collector who recently passed. I was able to convince the family to sell it to me instead of a dealer after I explained the situation," Jack explained.

I stood silent, unable to articulate everything I was feeling. It wasn't even about the comic itself. It was so much more. Jack had been quietly waiting, tracking the pieces I'd lost so long ago. That was more than friendship.

"I—I can't. I mean, I can, but—" The words lodged in my throat. I couldn't process everything I was feeling and speak at the same time.

Jack pulled me into a hug, holding me as I sobbed.

"Dude, it's okay," he said as he soothed me.

"It's not okay. My gift for you sucks in comparison," I said between fresh tears, trying to lighten the mood.

"I'm not Poppy. Gifting isn't a competition," he replied.

That made me laugh, easing some of the tension in my chest.

"She is kind of weird about gifts sometimes, isn't she?" I agreed.

Poppy didn't always have the tools to verbalize affection, so she communicated through other means—mostly gift giving. Unfortunately, it sometimes led her to being a bit competitive, using the gifts to prove she loved me more. It was an issue we were actively working on.

"Yeah," Jack said as he took a step back. "In fact, maybe don't tell her about the comic."

I smiled and nodded, not bothering to explain I hadn't planned to, anyway. Sentimental value aside, the comic was worth a pretty penny. The last thing I needed was Poppy insecure because she didn't spend as much as someone else. Or putting herself into debt to measure up.

And now to get it to the car without her seeing it.

Chapter 6
No Going Home

Poppy

"So...still in the honeymoon phase?" Sophie teased.

I rolled my eyes as I sipped the cranberry sprite mocktail she made me earlier. Normally, I wouldn't bother with the virgin drinks, but with a pub crawl later, I thought it was best I waited to get my booze on.

"You make it sound like we're a real couple," I said, more than a little annoyed.

"Aren't you, though? That's the arrangement, right?" she asked.

I stared at my drink and let out a sigh. Yes, the arrangement this time was the full experience, as Nixon called it, but it was still an act. He was getting the ideal girlfriend experience, not the real thing.

"Not exactly, and that's the problem. Nixon wants the rom-com relationship you see in the movies," I explained.

Sophie wrinkled her brow as she gave me a look.

"That sounds amazing! I wish Jack was like that," she said dreamily.

Was she being serious?

"No," I argued, "it sounds exhausting. I don't want to be *on* all the freaking time. That's part of why I hate the idea of settling down with someone long-term. The truth is, if Nixon and I dated, it wouldn't look any different from us as friends, except we'd share a bed and stop dating other people. That's not what he's looking for."

"Oh, Poppy," Sophie said, reaching out to console me.

I brushed her off, not wanting anyone's pity. It wasn't like I was actually sad about it. When I first started crushing on him, yeah, but we'd been together for over a decade by now. The mourning period of what would never be was long over.

"Don't, Soph. I'm fine with things the way they are. Besides, you can't break up if you were never really dating to begin with," I said.

At least that's what I kept telling myself.

"So this is where you lovely ladies have been hiding," Jack said as he entered the kitchen.

I stiffened for a fraction of a second, worried he overheard our conversation. Not that I said anything wrong, but I knew the situationship between Nixon and me was a point of contention for Jack.

Deep down, I couldn't help wondering if it was jealousy on his part. Being knocked down to best friend number two probably wasn't easy. Then again, I was the one that nursed Nixon through his break up with Ginny all those years ago. Where was Jack during that time? *Moving Sophie up here with him.*

I flashed him a tight smile.

"Just trying to get a moment alone with Sophie since you won't let her join us later for the pub crawl," I said sweetly.

Jack's smile never faltered. He was far too used to my attempts to bait him. It wasn't ever out of malice, just our dynamic. We shared the two most important people in our lives, so sometimes there was a power struggle. At the end of the day, I knew he came first with Sophie and that was fine. It was only fair since I was Nixon's number one.

"That can't be helped, Pops. My mom expects a full attendance on Christmas Eve *and* Christmas morning. You know how it goes," he said.

"That I do," I agreed.

Jack moved next to Sophie, pulling her into his embrace as he gave her an adorable little kiss on the top of her head. She giggled in response before turning back to face me. Clearly not wanting any distance between them, Jack kept her in his hold with her back flush against his chest.

Despite Sophie's earlier comment, it was clear they had the picture perfect relationship movies were made of.

And that sickeningly sweet picture was why I could never really hate Jack, not even when he almost ruined my Thanksgiving by putting stupid worries inside Nixon's head. He was great for Sophie so I had to love him.

"Actually, we were thinking of spending next Christmas with Sophie's family...in Florida." Jack gave me a look that was far from subtle. My mother would have been proud.

"I don't know—" I tried to push back, but the squeals of Sophie's excitement cut me off.

"Oh my God, yes!" she exclaimed. "You and Nixon should totally go, too! We could meet up while there. Maybe introduce Jack to your family?"

Record scratch. Wait, what?

"It would be nice to put faces to names when you and Nixon talk about them," Jack agreed.

No. No, it would not. Over the years, my family had grown quite attached to Nixon. As far as my siblings were concerned, he was one hundred percent one of us and they could be just as territorial as me. Meeting the man Nixon often described as "like a brother" would likely cause a bit of competitive tension between him and Jacob that I didn't want to deal with.

"Maybe," I said, not wanting to commit to anything.

It wasn't that I didn't want to go home and see my family, God knows I missed them, but a trip like that would take up a sizable amount of my vacation time. I banked that time for conventions and the occasional trip to go somewhere fun. That and going home wasn't as simple as it used to be.

Almost everyone now had families of their own. Zane was the only other one who wasn't married with kids. Don't get me wrong, I loved my nieces and nephews, but kids can be a lot. And there were six of them total between Amy, Jacob, and Fallon.

"Promise to at least think about it," Sophie pleaded.

I put on my best smile and nodded, not wanting to crush the hopeful twinkle in her eyes. I could wait until after Christmas to do that.

"So, where's Nixon?" I asked, desperate to veer the conversation to anywhere that wasn't Florida.

"Mingling," Jack said with a shrug. "Why? It's not like you two need to be attached at the hip. A little space is healthy."

I took a sharp inhale through my nose, slowly exhaling as I brought my drink to my lips. No one could push my buttons quite like Jack, and judging by the look on his face, it might have been intentional.

As much as I wanted to ask him what the fuck he meant, I knew better. It was Christmas Eve, and I was a guest in their home even if I spent enough time here to consider it a second home. Instead, I took a long, slow sip of my drink and watched the chaos unfold.

Sophie jerked herself out of her husband's hold, taking a couple steps back when he tried to reach for her. She looked pissed—a scowl on her face and one hand on her hip. Jack was such an idiot.

"Why the hell would you say that? What's wrong with you?" she snapped.

Surprisingly, Jack didn't seem fazed in the least. He reached out again for his wife, successfully pulling her back to him this time.

"What? Weren't you complaining just the other night that you haven't seen Poppy as much lately? I'm only looking out for my wife," he replied softly.

Sophie's eyes dropped to the floor as she stammered over her words.

"Yes, but that's—that's not what I meant. You made it sound so—"

Jack tilted her chin upward, silencing her lips with his. It was a sweet, tender moment between them until it wasn't. Sophie moaned as Jack deepened the kiss, his hands roaming toward her ass. That was more than I wanted to see so I quietly noped the hell out of the kitchen, leaving the two lovebirds alone.

Rejoining the festivities, I did a quick sweep of the dining room. No Nixon, but the food looked divine. Driven by a rumbly tummy and indecision, I grabbed a plate and piled it high with a little of everything.

Picking up one of the little sausages covered in barbeque sauce, I gave it a quick inspection before popping it in my mouth. My eyes closed, a soft moan escaping me as I savored the way the sweet and tangy flavors of the sauce blended with the savory sausage. *God, I love food.*

"I could listen to your moans all day," a familiar feminine voice whispered from behind.

Chapter 7
Blast from the Past

Poppy

Startled, I quickly swallowed my bite before turning to see someone I hadn't seen in a very long while.

"Fuck, Kylie! You startled me."

My eyes instantly dropped to Kylie's lips, painted with a cranberry lip stain that really popped against her pale skin, as she flashed me a wide smile. She looked the same as ever—jet black curls tied up in twin pigtails, porcelain skin, and the perfect smokey eye look I wished I could replicate.

"Yeah, I noticed," she replied with a devilish wink.

My cheeks burned as I tried to tell myself not to stare.

"Sorry. You know me and food," I said awkwardly. *That was stupid.*

Thankfully, Kylie didn't seem to think so. It was hard not to notice the way she was looking at me—like I was the dish she wanted to devour. Unfortunately, it didn't matter. Not that I wasn't interested. She was exactly my type—gorgeous, brash, stylish. Without thinking, I let my eyes wander over her curves, covered by the Krampus sweater dress she wore. *Definitely my type.*

Except she was Nixon's ex.

They dated for a bit shortly after we moved here and split on very good terms. They actually stayed friends, as far as I knew, but I always kept a little bit of distance after the split. It wasn't because I harbored any ill will. I just didn't trust myself not to do anything with her.

One boundary that Nixon and I had was to never date the other's exes. It was necessary to keep potential jealousy from souring the friendship.

Kylie was actually the reason for the rule. She was the first time one of us invited the other to be a third in the bedroom. She was also the first woman that I did more with than just kiss.

We were both flirty by nature, though Nixon never seemed to mind while they were dating. If anything, he seemed pleased by our friendliness with each other.

Nixon always loved when I was close with his partners, actually. I mean, I liked when he got along with my partners, too, but it wasn't quite the same. Looking back, he always seemed to want to integrate me into the relationship in some way. *Going to have to unpack that later.*

After the amicable split, I thought things would stay the same between Kylie and me. But then Nixon sat me down about a month after and expressed his desire to add the rule about exes.

He never outright said it was because of Kylie, but I could read between the lines.

After that, I kept her at arm's length. It sucked to lose a friend, but the fact that I couldn't trust myself around her made me question if I ever saw her as one and not a potential fuck. Kylie deserved better than that in her life.

Though, judging by the way her eyes kept dropping to my cleavage, I think we wanted the same things.

"Definitely digging that outfit. I half expected to see you in something louder after bumping into Nixon. I had forgotten about that sweater you got him," she said.

"Aren't his Christmas kittens the cutest?" I squealed.

Kylie chuckled as she shook her head. My stomach did a stupid little flip as her sparkling blue eyes met mine. The attraction was purely superficial by now, but fuck if it wasn't still there.

I watched in slow motion as she reached out, running a single finger down the sleeve of my sweater without breaking eye contact. I bit my lip as a shiver ran through me. All the memories of what she could do with a single finger flooded my mind.

"I've missed your energy, Poppy," she said seductively.

And just like that, I started drowning in guilt. Here I was making heart-eyes at some chick after promising Nixon I'd keep it in my pants. This was exactly why I knew I didn't deserve him.

Sensing my change in mood, Kylie frowned.

"Is everything okay?" she asked with a slight tilt of her head. The move was both adorable and sexy, which made the next two words completely necessary.

"Holiday pact," I answered.

Kylie's eyes widened.

"Oh! Fuck, Poppy. I'm sorry. I didn't mean to cross any lines. I just got so excited when I saw you—" She stumbled over her words, desperate to apologize.

"No, no. It's okay. How would you have known?" I said, trying to reassure her.

"True. The way Nixon and that big, broad ginger were talking, I just assumed that was his boyfriend," she confessed.

I stared at Kylie, blinking in confusion. Big, broad ginger? It took me a moment to register who she was talking about.

"Rupert?" I asked.

Kylie shrugged as she plucked one of my coveted mini sausages from my plate and took a small bite.

"I guess? I never got his name, but he was staring daggers at me while I had a quick chat with Nix," she said.

Kylie giggled as my face scrunched in displeasure. Here I was trying to be on my best behavior, and Nixon was flirting with his rugby crush. Excuse me, former crush, as he corrected me repeatedly. *Yeah, former crush, my ass.*

"Oh my God, are you jealous?" Kylie asked with way too much glee.

"No," I said, shaking my head. "Not jealous, frustrated."

She studied me for a moment before letting out a sigh. All the flirtatiousness faded from her eyes as what I could only describe as resignation set in.

"I see it now," she said, almost as if to herself.

"See what?" I asked.

Kylie shook her head dismissively, a dimmed smile pulling at her lips.

"Don't worry about it. Why don't we take a seat in the living room so you can actually eat your food while we catch up?" she suggested.

I was going to protest, but then my stomach rumbled loudly.

"Yeah, that's not a bad idea," I conceded.

Kylie grabbed my wrist and led me to the heart of the party while I wondered what she meant before.

Chapter 8
Boundaries

Nixon

I smiled politely as Rupert droned on excitedly about...something. It was hard to follow as the topic jumped from one sport to another. It started when I asked about the rugby league he was in and how it was going, but we somehow ended up talking about soccer—the real football, as he kept pointing out. *Yeah, don't care.* I started disassociating from the conversation soon after, briefly tuning in when I heard the word baseball because I had no idea how we got there.

I was not a sports fan. I knew a little bit about a lot of sports thanks to the men I was typically attracted to. But no sport held my interest, not even bowling despite Poppy's best efforts. The only reason I let her drag me to the lanes every few months was because of the beer and nachos her favorite spot served. That, and they had a pretty impressive arcade.

As if on cue, Poppy's laughter caught my attention, drowning out every other sound in the room. I glanced around, spotting her on the couch with Kylie, of all people. *Fucking great.*

I adored Kylie. She was one of only a handful of exes I stayed close to after the breakup. Nothing was wrong in the relationship, per se. We just wanted different things out of life at the time. I was still on the fence about things like marriage and children, while she knew for certain she was child-free for life. It felt disingenuous to continue the relationship knowing we might not end up on the same page about something so big. So, we parted as friends.

Then the questions started about Poppy. Until then, I never considered an ex might show an interest in her. I knew they were into each other while Kylie and I were dating, but that was different because I was still part of the equation. The thought of them together without me...I hated the way it made me feel.

You were the one that initiated things between them, I reminded myself. Yeah, but it was because I was being a good friend. Also, something about opening the relationship to include Poppy made sense. We were a package deal. If Kylie didn't have me, then she didn't get Poppy.

Rupert loudly cleared his throat, making his displeasure at my lack of attention known.

"Sorry," I mumbled.

Except I wasn't sorry. The apology was more of a reflex than anything. The truth was, I desperately wanted to be on the couch with Poppy instead of listening to Rupert droll on about shit that didn't interest me.

Rupert's face softened as he leaned closer. I shifted uncomfortably, my eyes falling to the floor as I prayed Poppy didn't look over. The last thing I needed was for her to misunderstand my current situation. Not that I thought she'd be jealous or anything. No, she'd be over the moon for me, graciously backing out of the pact.

Placing two fingers under my chin, Rupert guided my eyes back to his. I blushed for a fraction of a second from the intimate action before I remembered myself.

"She's having fun. You should, too," he said softly.

The swoony look in his eyes as he leaned a little closer made my stomach twist in knots. I needed to put a stop to this once and for all. It wasn't fair to anyone.

"Listen, Rupert. Poppy and I—"

"Have a little holiday pact of some sort. I know," he replied, completely unbothered.

I pulled back slightly, staring at him in confusion. People knew about our arrangement, but only our closest friends and maybe a few exes. It wasn't something we hid, but we didn't broadcast it either—especially the holiday pact since it rarely came into play.

Rupert let out a sigh and rolled his eyes.

"Jack told me after Thanksgiving. He said it's why you were acting so strange during the potluck," he explained.

"Then you understand why this is not appropriate?" I said, motioning between us.

Rupert stood upright, frustration clouding his features. If we weren't in a room full of people and I didn't know for certain that the large ginger was nothing more than a big teddy bear, I would have been nervous at the change in demeanor.

"What? She's allowed to play around and you're not?" he snapped, motioning toward Poppy on the couch.

I glanced towards her, grateful that she seemed oblivious to my fight. Poppy had a tendency to overcorrect if she thought she was in the way, which she never was. Thankfully, Rupert kept his voice low so only the people directly near us seemed aware of the scene unfolding.

"She's not playing around—" I tried to explain, but Rupert wouldn't listen.

"Open your eyes, Nixon. She's flirting with that girl."

Pausing to take a breath, I took a moment to calm myself.

Was Poppy flirting? Possibly. That was her personality. She wasn't the best at distinguishing the difference between flirty and friendly. It was all the same to her.

Was I jealous? A little, but not much. Poppy was loyal to me and our friendship. Even without the holiday pact, nothing was going to happen between her and Kylie.

Rupert knew neither of these points, which made me realize just how little he bothered to get to know Poppy since infiltrating our group of friends.

"That right there is why this will never happen," I finally said.

"Excuse me?" Rupert's eyes narrowed as he crossed his arms. The move was clearly some intimidation tactic, which was yet another mark against him. The fact that he handled rejection so poorly was a huge red flag.

"She is my best friend, the single most important person in my life. If you actually wanted to get with me, you would have made the effort to get to know her," I explained calmly.

"I have—" he tried to argue, but I didn't give him the chance.

"No, you haven't, or you'd know that nothing is going to happen between her and Kylie. I'm done being polite."

I turned before Rupert could respond and walked toward the couch, leaving him standing there with a shocked look on his face. I'd be lying if I said it didn't give me a little thrill to shut him down the way I did.

Feeling a wave of confidence, I marched toward the couch with every intention of claiming what was mine.

Poppy and Kylie took notice as I approached. Their once boisterous laughter dimmed into mischievous giggles as they looked between each other and then back to me. The two really were similar in a lot of ways. That was probably what drew me to Kylie in the first place—a decent imitation of the woman I loved. But she wasn't Poppy. No one but Poppy was Poppy.

"Hello, ladies," I greeted.

"Hello, again. We were wondering how long before you decided to join us," Kylie taunted.

Poppy patted the empty spot to her left, which I was more than happy to occupy. Sliding next to my bestie on the couch, I threw my arm around her, enjoying the way her body relaxed against mine. It all felt so natural.

"It looked like you were having a wonderful time," Poppy teased.

The look in her eyes as she looked up at me said she knew that I was, in fact, not having a wonderful time. That meant that she had been watching my conversation with Rupert and chose not to intervene. That wasn't like Poppy at all. Normally, she'd rush to my rescue when a social interaction was going south.

Part of me wanted to be concerned by her weird behavior and call it out, but the other part of me didn't want to risk a fight when she was currently cozy in my hold.

"So much fun. I think I have a new appreciation for sport-ball," I replied dryly.

Poppy snorted in amusement before picking a piece of food off her plate and popping it in her mouth. At least someone was amused.

"I never understood why you chase after the meatheads. It's not like you have anything in common with them," Kylie remarked.

I sat dumbfounded, unsure how to respond. Having to defend my dating preferences was not something I planned on doing today.

"You don't need to have anything in common to have fun in the bedroom. Sometimes you just want a big, strong idiot that can toss you around and fuck your brains out," Poppy said wistfully.

Kylie gave me a sympathetic look. All I could do was flash her a weak smile while pretending Poppy's words weren't a punch to the gut. I was in pretty peak condition myself, but I wasn't tossing anyone around.

But you do like to be tossed around, I reminded myself.

"Anyway—" I said, trying to veer the conversation in a new direction.

"What? Don't act like that's not what you're into. Our walls are not that thick. I hear things," Poppy stated.

And once again, I was left speechless. I mean, I knew our walls weren't soundproof, but I always put on noise canceling headphones or something if I was home while Poppy was getting freaky. I always assumed she did the same.

"You hear things, or you're purposely listening in?" Kylie asked.

That...that wasn't a bad question.

She leaned closer to Poppy, eyes sparkling with mischief as she waited for an answer. As much as I hated to admit it, I was equally curious. I mean, I should have been angry. Listening to me with my partners was a clear violation of boundaries, but I couldn't deny the thrill the thought gave me.

"Naughty, naughty, Kylie. I'm not going to discuss my masturbation habits out in the open," Poppy replied playfully.

That was a confession. A really hot confession judging by the way my dick was now uncomfortably pressing into my jeans.

Kylie seemed as surprised as I was, her eyes raised as she looked to me for guidance on how to respond. I was absolutely no help, my mind lost in a sea of images of Poppy pleasuring herself to the sounds of me getting railed in another room. Her body writhing on her bed with a hand between her thighs as she times her climax to meet mine—

Achievement Unlocked: New Kink

There was no way I was going to be able to hold a conversation with the porno currently playing in my head. I needed release, and I needed it now.

"Excuse us," I said.

Without giving Poppy a chance to fight back, I swiftly grabbed her plate and placed it on the table before standing and dragging her away from the main party.

Chapter 9

Show Me

Poppy

Sometimes I say stupid things without thinking. Things like admitting I may have pleasured myself occasionally while listening to Nixon get bent over and fucked hard in the other room.

He was obviously pissed by the way he abruptly ended the conversation with Kylie. At least he was taking me somewhere private to scold me. It would have been twice as embarrassing if he did it in front of everyone.

Like you did in front of Kylie.

I cringed internally, unsure why I said any of it out loud. I was trying to pretend I wasn't jealous of Rupert because a good friend doesn't get jealous. Except I was jealous.

The rational part of me knew there was nothing to be jealous of. Every time I glanced over, Nixon looked completely spaced out and disinterested. It was honestly impressive that Rupert didn't notice.

But the conversation kept going, and I began to wonder if I was the clueless one.

Once Nixon joined us on the couch, I knew I was right and a tiny bit of guilt set in. When Kylie made her little jab, I felt the need to defend him. Only I took it way too far.

And now I'm being dragged off somewhere so he can tell me just how inappropriate I was.

My heart raced as we approached the spare room. I hated when people were mad at me, like really mad at me. Especially Nixon. He would get really quiet and distant. Nothing was worse than the person you loved most pulling away from you.

As soon as we entered the room, I sucked in a deep breath and prepared to grovel. Maybe if I was sincere enough, he'd forgive me and we could move on. I mean, Nixon had known me for long enough—he knew I sometimes said shit without thinking. Surely he'd take that into consideration.

He reached out—one hand firmly on my hips, the other fisting my hair. His grip was tight, almost to the point of pain, as he stared at me with an expression I couldn't decipher. The move was more than a bit shocking since Nixon was never prone to physical aggression.

Deep down, I knew he wouldn't actually hurt me, but that didn't stop the panic from taking over. My breathing picked up as my heart matched its pace. I needed to beg for forgiveness, and I needed to do it fast.

"Listen, Nixon, I'm—"

The apology cut short as his mouth crashed onto mine. My body froze for a split second as my mind rushed to make sense of the sudden turn of events. Nixon wasn't mad. He was...horny? Really horny, judging by the hard bulge poking into my hip and the way he was desperately trying to devour my mouth.

Yay?

Still a little in shock, I grabbed onto Nixon's arms and slowly returned his affection. He hummed in appreciation as his tongue probed further.

The longer we kissed, the more frenzied he became. The kiss devolved into something messy and chaotic while he dry-humped me like a sex-crazed teenager. It was a side of Nixon I'd never experienced, so lost to his carnal needs that I was sure he was going to come in his pants—and I fucking loved it.

Finally breaking for air, Nixon rested his forehead on mine. His grip on my hair was still tight like he was still struggling to maintain control.

"God, we are so fucked up sometimes," he said between panting breaths.

Of all the things I expected him to say, that was not one of them.

"I don't disagree," I said cautiously.

He wasn't wrong. We were both little freaks in our own way, but we didn't usually have conversations surrounding the confrontation and deconstruction of our issues in the middle of sexy times. It was kind of a mood killer, to be honest.

"I can't believe you listen in like a little pervert," he murmured.

"I'm not a little pervert!" I snapped defensively.

I hated that word. It carried such a negative connotation. Liking sex and kinky shit didn't mean there was something wrong with me.

Nixon finally released me, allowing me to stumble back a few steps. A smile curved the corners of his mouth as his eyes pinned me with a mischievous stare.

I wanted to be mad, but the way he watched me as I slowly walked backwards was doing things to my body. My poor little thong was already soaked through. Nixon wasn't usually one to give chase, but in that moment I knew there was no escaping.

"You are a little pervert, and it's hot. Now get on the bed and show me," he commanded.

"Show you?" I asked, more than a bit confused. How was I supposed to show him how I eavesdropped?

"Yes. Lift your skirt and show me how you touch yourself when you're listening in," he instructed.

Closing the gap between us, Nixon grabbed my hips and walked me backward until the back of my legs hit the bed. I was barely aware that he was lifting me onto the bed, my head still reeling from his request.

"Here? At Jack and Sophie's? But we don't fuck at Jack and Sophie's," I tried to reason. It was one of the few rules we had while at their house.

"I'm not asking you to fuck. I'm telling you to play with that pretty pussy of yours while I watch," he countered.

I stared at him for a moment as I contemplated giving in.

The "No Fucking at Jack and Sophie's Rule" was more of an unspoken one. It was about manners and decency. You don't go rubbing your naked body on other people's furniture.

On the other hand, I wouldn't be naked. I could let Nixon watch me masturbate without removing a single stitch of clothing. And like he said, we wouldn't be fucking.

Nixon's eyes dropped down to my hands as I reached for the hem of my skirt. His eyes burned with a dark fire as he watched me slowly raise the plaid fabric, exposing myself.

"Another thong?" he asked with amusement.

"I thought it would be useful," I replied with a smile.

Nixon's eyes briefly met mine as he smirked before nodding in approval.

With my skirt in one hand and my thighs spread open, I reached down with the other. My fingers delicately traced the barely there patch of red lace that covered my pussy as a small moan escaped my lips.

Nixon said he wanted to see how I touched myself when I listened in, but I knew what he really wanted. It was what every guy wanted—performative masturbation. You know, the stuff you see in pornos. Honestly, after watching my fair share of them, it was no wonder most men had no idea how a woman's nether regions worked.

Closing my eyes, I focused on the movements of my fingers as I ran them up and down the lace. I was more of a tiny circles girl, but the movement wasn't nearly dramatic enough for what we were doing.

"Where did you go?" Nixon asked.

"Sorry," I said, opening my eyes. "I was just picturing you with Bryce."

Nixon's eyes narrowed, locking in on my face. He studied me with suspicion, filling me with enough unease that I had to look away.

"You're lying," he said with a sternness that sent a shiver down my spine.

"No. The last time I listened in was you and Bryce. I was just trying to channel that moment," I explained.

Nixon wrapped his fingers around my throat. The light pressure of his hold felt like a collar. He was claiming me as his, taking control.

I swallowed, the action proving difficult with his fingers restricting me. It was a show of power that made me melt in his hold. Any resistance I still held onto dissipated, and I submitted completely to him.

"I don't doubt that was the last time you eavesdropped, but that's not where your head was just now," he said, his voice laced with a hint of danger. He was angry.

Nixon tightened his hold on me, forcing out the neediest whine in response. I wanted more. I wanted it all. I wanted him to break me down and make me beg. I wanted him to take everything he wanted, using me like a toy.

"And I *know* how you fucking touch yourself, Poppy," he all but growled.

His other hand moved between my thighs, his knuckles trailing over my lace thong. I whimpered in response, my hips bucking involuntarily in search of more friction.

"It's something like this, right?" he taunted.

His thumb pressed lightly on my clit through the fabric as he moved it in a tight circular motion. I sucked in a sharp breath, my muscles tensing as sparks of pleasure coursed through my body.

"There we go. That's the real thing," Nixon cooed softly as he continued to tease me. "Now talk. Tell me what you heard and how it made you so damn needy that you had to fuck your hand."

I blushed, overwhelmed by everything—the filthy words, his hand on my throat, his thumb on my clit. My hands fisted the comforter underneath me as I tried to ground myself enough to think. Nixon wanted me to talk. I need to talk.

Closing my eyes, I tried to remember that night. It had been so long ago—long before Cherry.

Bryce was big, like Rupert—broad shoulders, solid chest, thighs like tree trunks. One time he flexed for me, and I needed both hands to wrap around his biceps. He was built.

Opening my eyes, I stared straight into Nixon's and began to lay the scene.

"You thought I was sleeping, but I was wide awake. You weren't being very quiet. It sounded like you two were going at it right outside my room."

Nixon chuckled, the look in his eyes saying I wasn't far off. "Oops."

"I remember you whimpering. I was actually kind of jealous because I've never made you whimper like that. It was so hot," I confessed.

Nixon slipped a finger past my thong, lining it with my entrance but not pressing in. He was so close to filling me it slowly drove me insane, but I knew better than to disobey. Instead, I sat perfectly still and endured the sweet torture of his dominance.

"Then what?" he asked. His demeanor was calm and collected, but I saw the hunger in his eyes as he commanded me to continue.

Closing my eyes once more, I focused, trying to remember every detail I could.

"He started fingering you. I remember because he kept talking about how tight you were. The noises you were making—I reached between my thighs and started to play with myself while I listened. He made you beg to suck him off. You kept saying 'please, sir'. I think he called you *pet*?"

Submissive Nixon was nothing new to me. I'd been witness to others commanding him, having done it myself plenty of times, but the way Bryce spoke to him that night was different. It sounded more raw than anything we'd ever done. I had definitely never heard Nixon say *sir* outside of work.

"I remember that night," he said quietly.

I opened my eyes to find him staring at me through hooded lids, his eyes glazed over like he was lost in a dream.

"He edged you until you were in tears, begging—for his release, not yours," I continued. "You were so desperate to taste him. I came twice while listening."

Nixon's eyes widened, his throat bobbing as he swallowed.

"How the fuck are you so damn perfect?" he asked.

"I—what?" I said, stumbling over my words as a fresh blush crept its way over my face.

"I'm going to taste you now. Try not to be too loud. They have a full house."

Chapter 10

Getting Frisky in the Guestroom

Nixon

Releasing my hold on Poppy, I dropped to my knees and nipped at her inner thigh. She squeaked and tried to pull back, but I quickly grabbed both thighs and held her in place.

I had all but forgotten about that night with Bryce until she started recounting it for me.

That relationship had been...intense, but the sex was always amazing. One time we even included Poppy in the bedroom. He made her come over and over until she was sobbing for a break. Then he made me kneel between her thighs on the bed and stroked my cock, painting her body with my cum while he fingered my ass.

I couldn't remember what led to us getting down to business in the hallway, but I do remember being insanely desperate to suck every last drop from him. Knowing Poppy had been listening the whole time and secretly having her own fun made me ache to hear her make those noises now.

"Fuck, Poppy," I rasped as I moved her thong to the side, "do you have any fucking idea what you do to me?"

I licked up her slick slit, enjoying the way she squirmed and moaned. She tasted like heaven wrapped in an orgasm.

"Fuck. Nixon," Poppy whined as her hips bucked. God, she was needy for me, no longer able to keep her body under control.

"No, no fucking right now. Instead, I'm going to edge this sweet pussy until you're ready to break," I taunted.

Making good on my word, I slipped two fingers inside her warm, wet cunt and began thrusting while my tongue lavished her clit with attention. She was already so worked up that it was easy to bring her to the edge of the cliff, but that wasn't enough.

I kept my focus, ignoring the throbbing erection that screamed for attention, waiting for that perfect moment. As soon as the telltale signs presented, I pulled my fingers out and stood up, denying her the sweet relief her body yearned for. Her pleasure was mine to control.

"What. The. Fuck?" Poppy growled.

My ferocious little brat glared at me with the fury of a wild animal scorned. She was pissed, and for some strange reason that turned me on more.

"I never said I'd let you finish. Now, drop to your knees," I ordered.

Unfastening my jeans, I pulled out my cock and gave it a few strokes. Unsurprisingly, Poppy stayed on the bed, staring daggers in my direction.

"Whatever I want, whenever I want. No pushback," I reminded her.

She silently stared at me for another few seconds before pushing off the bed and dropping to her knees as I asked.

"Don't think I won't get my revenge," she warned.

I couldn't help laughing. That was such a Poppy thing to say. She scowled at me from the floor like a fierce kitten. As adorable as she was, she definitely had claws that I would have to contend with later.

"I'm sure you will, but not today. You are mine to do whatever I want with until the end of the day. And right now, I want to fuck your face."

Poppy reached out to grab the base of my shaft, but I swatted her hand away. That wasn't what I was looking for. I was on a special kind of high, savoring the power I had over my friend.

"Hands behind your back, Pops. I told you I'm fucking your face."

She gave a little huff as she folded her hands behind her back. The look in her eyes only confirmed I was definitely in for it later.

Grabbing a fistful of her hair, I held her head firmly in place as I pushed my cock past her beautiful red lips. She parted them willingly, letting me slide into her warm, wet heat.

Her mouth felt good. Too fucking good.

I should have been more careful, or mindful of how much Poppy could take, but I didn't care. I was too worked up not to fuck her mouth like she was some toy because, in that moment, she was. My toy, and meant only for my pleasure.

I fucked her sweet mouth like a man possessed. I needed to come, to fill her mouth with my release, and make her swallow every drop. It was all I could think about.

Poppy took it all like a champ despite the gagging and tears streaming down her face. There was no struggle or attempt to escape. No, she knelt obediently, letting me use her. It was so damn hot I couldn't stop myself from tumbling over the edge.

My orgasm came crashing over me with unexpected force. It all happened so fast that I didn't have a chance to warn Poppy before I emptied my load into her mouth. She tried to pull back, but I held her in place. It wasn't every day I got Poppy to drink me down, so the opportunity wasn't going to waste.

"Nuh-uh, Pops. Be a good girl and swallow. All of it. Do not waste a single fucking drop," I commanded.

Poppy looked up at me with a glazed expression as she did exactly as told. *Interesting*. It wasn't every day that Poppy conceded to swallowing. She was being much more compliant than usual.

Then a dark thought crept its way into my brain as I wondered just how compliant Poppy really was. It was wrong to even consider taking advantage of her in such a state, but the opportunity was too tempting to pass up.

"Marry me, Poppy." Three little words—the same request after every blow job, but for the first time I held real hope.

Poppy watched me from the floor—eyes glazed over and a drop of cum on her lips. She was an absolute vision.

"If I didn't love you so much, I'd teach you a lesson and say yes," she said with a warmth that didn't match the rejection she just threw at me.

Her response left me utterly dumbfounded. What in the hell was that supposed to mean?

Teach me a lesson. Teach me all the damn lessons! Please!

I wanted to scream out in protest, but I swallowed the words down. Arguing wouldn't do anything other than ruin an otherwise perfect moment. Instead, I did what I always did and pretended I wasn't dying inside.

Reaching down, I offered Poppy a helping hand. Once standing in front of me, I noticed her eyes were slightly smudged from the tears, though her lipstick was still mostly intact.

"Your eyes...they're a little—" I reached toward her face, but she took a step back.

"It's okay. I can sneak into Sophie's stash and clean it up. She doesn't mind," Poppy said.

I gave her a soft smile, my eyes dropping once again to her lips.

"Will that lipstick come off later?"

She gave me an unconcerned shrug that didn't fill me with confidence.

"We'll see tonight."

Chapter 11
An Awkward Friendship

Poppy

I sat in front of Sophie's gorgeous oak vanity, carefully touching up my eye makeup. It really wasn't that bad, but I also wasn't in the mood for whispers after disappearing together so obviously. Maybe if Nixon had let me finish I wouldn't have cared, but now I was in a strange mood. Being edged with no release does that to a person.

"Hey, Pops," Jack greeted, immediately putting me on edge. *Fuck.*

My cheeks flushed with embarrassment and a dash of guilt as I realized how bad the situation probably looked—wife's bestie alone in your bedroom, rummaging through your wife's things.

"Fuck, Jack! I'm sorry! I wasn't thinking. I just needed to reapply some makeup, and I didn't have any makeup wipes, or eyeliner—"

Jack raised a hand, cutting my apology short.

"It's okay, Pops. I was just checking in on you to make sure you're okay. Nixon's parading around like the big man on campus with a shit-eating grin...or should I say pussy-eating grin?" he said, trying to reassure me.

I cringed internally. If Jack knew, then others probably did as well.

It was one thing to constantly sneak off at home, but at someone else's was completely different. I didn't want people worried about Nixon and me possibly fucking at their homes if they invited us over. It was rude on so many levels.

"Ugh, I'm sorry," I said. What else could I say?

Jack took a seat on the large bed behind me, his reflection staring at me through the mirror.

"Why are you sorry? Stop apologizing. We know you two fuck," he said with a smile.

I turned to face Jack directly. If he was trying to comfort me, he was doing a shit job of it. While I wasn't ashamed of my sexual appetite, I also didn't want to be reduced to the always horny girl who couldn't control herself.

"Not here. Never here," I said firmly.

Jack gave me a doubtful look, his mouth curving into a lopsided frown.

"You don't have to lie. No one is judging you," he said.

If that was true, then why did it feel like I was being judged? More so, I was being branded a liar, and why? Because the thought of me not thinking with my pussy was apparently ridiculous.

"I'm not lying. This is the first time we've fooled around like that here," I said defensively.

Jack blinked in disbelief before raising a hand to scratch the back of his head.

"Really? Fuck. Then I owe Sophie a really expensive dinner," he replied.

I turned back to the mirror and hastily finished up before putting everything away. Maybe it was the mood I was in, but I didn't like hearing that Jack and Sophie were taking bets on whether or not Nixon and I fucked around in their spare room. At least Sophie seemed to have my back.

"Well, I'm done. So, I'll see you back out there," I said as I rose to my feet.

Jack grabbed my wrist as I tried to retreat, holding me in place.

"Or you could chill in here for a moment. I know you don't like to be completely alone, so I can stay, too," he offered.

I froze, taking a moment to study Jack—like really study him. He seemed sincere in his offer, which only confused me more. After a few seconds, I decided to accept and retook my seat, if for no other reason than curiosity.

"Are *you* okay?" I asked.

Maybe this was a cry for help masked as concern for me. Not that Jack ever gave off toxic masculinity, men don't cry vibes, but I also never saw him particularly vulnerable.

Jack released his hold on me and smiled, seemingly happy that I decided to take him up on his offer to hide away for a little bit.

"I'm perfectly fine. Not exactly thrilled for Christmas lunch tomorrow. Aunt Karen keeps asking when I'm going to contribute to the next generation since everyone else already has, but aside from that, I'm fine," he replied.

I scrunched my face in displeasure. Family like that was the bane of my existence.

"You have one of those in the family, too?" I said.

"A few, actually. That's part of why we always spend Thanksgiving at your place. I'm not subjecting Sophie to that shit two holidays back to back," he explained.

"Well, if everything is fine, then why are we hiding out in here?" I asked point blank.

Jack chuckled.

"Because I know you. He's hovering, and that's not your thing, but you would never tell him that," he said.

I narrowed my gaze. This conversation was heading in a direction I did not care for. Jack needed to tread lightly because neither Sophie nor Nixon was around to keep me from speaking my mind.

"Don't even. I didn't mean it like that, so you can stop twisting my words in your little head," he said sternly.

I continued to stare him down in silence until his shoulders slumped and a long, drawn-out sigh escaped him.

"Believe it or not, I care about your happiness as much as his," he said dejectedly.

"Is that so?" I challenged.

I didn't believe that for one second. Yes, we were friends, but only because of Nixon and Sophie. There was nothing particularly wrong with Jack. He was a wonderful guy, but we were like oil and water. Over the years, we had turned the underlying tension into a sort of teasing friendship, but I could never see myself chilling one-on-one with the guy...which was probably why I felt so on edge at the moment.

"Yes, that is so," he snapped back with a hint of attitude.

An awkward silence fell between us, and for the first time, I wondered if maybe I misjudged our dynamic. *Was I the problem?* It wouldn't be the first time.

"I'm actually rooting for you two," Jack finally said.

I raised an eyebrow. There was no way that was true, but I didn't say anything, curious to see if he'd elaborate.

"Oh, whatever Poppy. I think you two would be great together if you both could get your heads out of your asses. But what I think doesn't matter. And I see the way you are looking at me, but I'm going somewhere with this. I swear," he said.

"Really? Because you are taking forever to get there," I teased.

Jack smiled before his expression faded to something more serious.

"It's okay to tell him no. He won't fall apart. Not for long, anyway," he replied.

"I'll keep that in mind," I said.

"No you won't, but I had to try. Like I said, I care about your happiness, too. If you want something more, we both know he'd jump at the chance...but that doesn't mean you have to just to make him happy."

With that little nugget of wisdom, Jack stood and walked out of the bedroom, leaving me to unpack everything that was said.

Chapter 12
Eye on the Prize

Nixon

After dropping off the car back home, we grabbed a Lyft and headed out to the first bar of the evening—Champagne and Sherry Delights. I wasn't exactly looking forward to a late afternoon bar crawl on Christmas Eve, but there was a prize that Poppy desperately wanted to win, so I didn't have much of a choice.

The whole idea of a Christmas Eve bar crawl was ridiculous to me. While I wasn't particularly into the holiday season, many were. I couldn't imagine anyone working tonight wouldn't rather be home with their families. Instead, they were stuck dealing with drunks who had nowhere better to be.

Poppy sat next to me, dancing in her seat to Mariah Carey's big Christmas anthem. It was one of her favorite songs, which meant it, along with the rest of the album, was part of the regular rotation this time of year. *All I want for Christmas is to go home and cuddle,* I thought dryly.

The music died down, fading into the next song—something slightly familiar that sounded like Britney Spears. Poppy snuggled into my side as she hummed along, a content smile on her face. That softened my mood considerably. I wrapped an arm around her, enjoying the way she felt against me.

"Are you two doing that pub crawl thing tonight?" the driver asked.

He was a young man with blond hair, blue eyes, and a slender build like mine. It was surprising he was striking up a conversation now when he had remained fairly quiet most of the ride.

"You know it. I got my eye on the grand prize," Poppy replied excitedly.

The grand prize. For five bucks, you got a stamp card for the bar crawl. Each of the five establishments taking part in the event had a special holiday cocktail just for the occasion. If you ordered the special drink, you got your card stamped. All five stamps entered you into a drawing. The grand prize was two tickets to the Bear and Brown Hotel's swanky New Year's Eve Bash, something I was not interested in at all.

The Bear and Brown Hotel was very upscale, and their New Year's Eve Bash was black tie. Tickets started at $150 a person, which was well more than I wanted to spend just to be in an uncomfortable suit while I eat pretentious hors d'oeuvres and drink overpriced wine. Even if the tickets were free, I couldn't see myself going. The whole thing sounded like a miserable time to me. Poppy, on the other hand, was practically frothing at the mouth to go.

"Do you have any plans?" I asked the driver. Not that I really cared, but it seemed like the polite thing to ask.

"Sure do. I'll probably take a few more rides after you two, then I'm heading home to my wife and daughter. It's Aubrey's first Christmas," he explained as he tapped a small photo of a baby that was taped to his center console.

"She's precious!" Poppy gushed as she leaned forward.

The driver looked a bit young to be a dad, but maybe that was my denial of my own age speaking. I was only a few years from forty, but I still felt like I was barely out of my twenties. Either way, I made a mental note to tip extra on the app when we arrived.

Poppy continued the conversation for the remainder of our ride, learning all about little Aubrey and how her first Christmas had gone so far. It was bittersweet to listen knowing that I'd likely never have kids of my own at this point. Not that I wanted kids, but I didn't not want them either.

If the right person had come along, I would have been down to procreate. But now I was pushing forty and had no desire to start a family so late in life. There was a time when I considered asking Poppy if she'd be down to make a kid, but she was staunchly child-free. At least we had plenty of nieces and nephews.

When the car pulled up to Champagne and Sherry Delights, there was already a small crowd gathered outside. It should have been a comfort that I was far from the only one without family on Christmas Eve, but I had Poppy. I didn't need to mingle amongst the other lost souls.

"Looks like we aren't the only ones who decided to start here," I said, failing to hold back my annoyance.

Poppy gave me a nudge as she flashed a smile. It was hard to stay in a sour mood when she was so happy.

"At least the others are holding us a table," she replied.

Stepping inside the bar, I was immediately taken aback by how pink everything was. The walls were a dusty rose, lined with mirrors of different shapes and sizes in some weird attempt at modern decor gone horribly wrong. The Christmas decorations were just as ghastly—a bubblegum pink Christmas tree with silver tinsel, a hot pink furry wreath, and nutcrackers that looked like they were better suited as extras in a Barbie movie.

"This place looks so cool! Maybe we should come here more often," Poppy said with excitement.

I cringed. *Like hell we will.*

Normally, we frequented dive bars or establishments geared toward our interests. The main things I looked for were a fun atmosphere or cheap booze, and I could already tell this place had neither.

"Hello! Welcome to Santa's Little Bar Crawl at Champagne and Sherry Delights!" the hostess greeted as we approached.

She was a curvy redhead with vibrant green eyes dressed in a sexy little elf costume that hugged her in all the right places. *Nice.* I turned to Poppy, expecting her to also be enjoying the view, only to see a tight smile stretched over her lips.

"Hi. Our friends are already here waiting on us," Poppy said with a slight edge to her voice.

I shifted uncomfortably, not sure what was happening. The hostess was totally Poppy's type, which meant that she should have been flirting, not staring the poor woman down with a fake smile like she was fighting the urge to stab her. *Maybe we'll be going home early after all.*

"Okay. Well, have you purchased your Santa's Little Bar Crawl stamp card yet?" the hostess asked. Her friendly expression looked strained as she spoke, her eyes darting between us cautiously.

Stepping forward, I donned my best smile and took over the conversation. The last thing we needed was a confrontation with the staff at the very first bar.

"No, we have not...Joy," I said, glancing down at her name tag. "Do we get that from you?"

I wasn't trying to flirt, but it was clear my attempt at friendliness was misunderstood as Joy leaned forward while not so subtly pressing her tits together. Mindful that Poppy was standing next to me, quite literally, I kept my eyes on Joy's eyes, knowing better than to let them trail south.

"Your server will supply them, cash only. But if there's anything else you need—"

"Nope, we're good," Poppy said as she grabbed my arm and forcefully pulled me along.

I should have been pissed at Poppy's behavior, or at the very least concerned that she thought the hostess was a threat when I only had eyes for her, but I was grinning like a goddamn fool as she dragged me across the bar.

"You're cute when you're jealous," I said, unable to stop myself.

It was true. Her face was flushed, her brow furrowed in frustration, and all because someone made an advance on me.

Poppy froze in the middle of the bar, her grip on my arm tightening. The look of anger in her eyes when she turned to face me should have scared me, but strangely, it made me hard as a rock.

"Jealous? You think I'm jealous of *her*?" she whisper-yelled over the noise of the crowd.

"Yeah. You have no reason to be, obviously, but I kinda dig this side of you," I replied.

"God, you're such an ass sometimes. *You're* the one who said no flirting. I didn't realize eye-fucking hostesses didn't count!" she shot back.

I bristled at the accusation. Being jealous that someone else was taking notice of me was one thing, but to think that I would be the one with the wandering eyes was a different beast entirely. I had spent the last month trying to show Poppy what we could be if she'd give me the chance. The fact that she thought I would stray so easily was insulting.

"I wasn't eye-fucking her. And since when do you care? You're normally the one who points the hotties out," I snapped. I didn't mean to snap, but the way she pushed my buttons sometimes made it hard.

Poppy folded her arms and glared at me, but I didn't back down. The fact that she doubted me was bad enough, but the hypocrisy of her accusation was an insult to injury.

"That's different," she insisted.

"How?" I challenged, raising a brow.

Her face scrunched in frustration as she stared back at me in silence. I loved Poppy, but she could be so damn stubborn sometimes. She knew I was right, but it was clear her pride wasn't going to let her admit it.

Only one thing to do.

Grabbing Poppy's hips, I pulled her body flush against mine. From the corner of my eyes, I could see some of the other patrons taking notice of our little scene. *An audience, perfect.*

"What if I make it clear who I belong to? Will that make you feel better?" I asked.

Without waiting for Poppy to answer, I leaned down and kissed her. Her lips parted easily, letting my tongue slide past all her defenses. She melted instantly, her body surrendering to mine.

A few whistles and cheers came from the surrounding tables, but I didn't care. That was the point, after all. I was offering a public claiming so everyone would know without a shadow of a doubt who I was there with.

When I pulled back, Poppy stood for a moment with eyes closed and a soft smile. When she finally opened her eyes, she had a dazed expression that matched the faint blush painting her cheeks. Mission accomplished.

Reaching down, I laced our fingers together before giving her a quick kiss on the cheek.

"Come on, Pops. Let's join the others," I said as I pulled her to the back where our friends were waiting.

Chapter 13
Getting Cozy

Poppy

If all the drinks for the bar crawl were as wonderful as what was served at Champagne and Sherry Delights, then I was going to have a great night. Not only did the white wine cocktail—amusingly named Cockin' Around the Christmas Tree—taste amazing, but it had a tall spring of rosemary sticking out of the middle like a little tree.

I carefully examined my now empty glass, trying to figure out how they got the spring of rosemary to stay in. There was clearly a layer of something on the bottom, maybe glue? Were they special glasses manufactured for this purpose? The longer I stared, the more I became intrigued.

The quickest way to get my answer was to reach in and touch the bottom, but I was too sober to get away with such weird behavior.

As if reading my mind, Nixon leaned in and whispered the answer.

"That's ice on the bottom." His warm breath against the shell of my ear sent a welcome shiver down my spine.

"Hm?" I murmured as I turned to face him, trying to play it cool.

He smirked before grabbing the glass from my hand and pointing to the bottom.

"That's the ice. They froze the water around the rosemary to keep it in place," he explained.

Mystery solved. Though it should have been obvious since the bottom was significantly colder than the rest of the glass. *Way to use your brain, Poppy.* Though that didn't explain how they got it to stay upright before the water was frozen.

"And what makes you think I wanted to know?" I asked playfully.

"The whole table could tell by the way you were staring at your glass," Percy interjected from across the table.

I scowled in his direction, but the big, broad rugby player with sandy brown hair was completely unbothered, winking at me in response. *Ass.*

Overall, I liked Percy. He was a bit of a sarcastic ass, but none of it was ever in malice. In fact, he was usually the first one to shut shit down if someone was crossing the line into cruel territory. He was also the one who brought Rupert into the fold—something I was less fond of as of late.

Next to Percy, Rupert scoffed, the action dripping with condescension.

"The first drink hit you that hard, Poppy?" he teased in a less than friendly manner.

Percy nudged his friend as he shook his head, admonishing him for going too far. *Like you weren't the one who started it*, I thought to myself. Rupert only rolled his eyes, clearly feeling no remorse for trying to pick a fight.

Whatever. I knew why Rupert was acting out. It was the same reason he had been shooting me dirty looks since I sat down. I had something he wanted...and maybe if he wasn't such an ass, I wouldn't have been so petty.

With a smile on my lips, I lean over and plant a kiss on Nixon's lips. I could feel his smile against my lips as he hummed in appreciation. He flashed me a gentle smile as we parted, his expression slightly dazed.

Kylie cleared her throat, pulling the attention away from Nixon and me. Her lips were drawn in a tight smile as she looked everywhere but us. Oops.

"I think everyone is done with their drinks. Should we settle our tabs and move on?" she asked the group. Not the smoothest transition under the circumstances, but it worked.

Only about half of the group agreed it was time to move on, Nixon and me included. As much as I was enjoying the vibe of the place, we had four more bars to hit followed by an evening full of Christmas movies. I didn't have time to waste.

In the end, Nixon and I were joined by Percy, Rupert, Kylie, and my two friends from work—Mari and Quinn. I had hoped Rupert was going to stay behind with the others, but luck was not on my side. He was unsurprisingly attached to Percy, who was currently staring at Quinn with hearts in his eyes.

When we arrived at Spruce, the rustic country bar, there were still plenty of open tables, much to my surprise. According to the sign up front, it was a seat yourself situation, so we grabbed a big round booth off to the side.

Percy thought he was being slick by slipping into the booth right after Quinn, but I wasn't the only one to notice. Mari paused and scowled before sliding in next to him, clearly perturbed to be separated from her bestie.

Nixon squeezed in next to Mari, pulling me along with him. Before I could get settled, he was pulling me into his lap, securing me in place with his arm around my waist.

"Really?" I huffed under my breath.

It wasn't that I didn't want to be close to Nixon, but we were in a giant, round booth sandwiched between five other people. It wasn't really the time or the place, even if his lap was surprisingly comfortable.

Nixon responded by pulling back my hair and trailing kisses down my neck. Goosebumps broke out over my body as my nipples hardened under my bra. Not wanting the rest of the table to catch on to my sudden arousal, I grabbed the tri-fold off the center of the table and tried to focus.

Unbothered by my lack of reaction, Nixon rested his chin on my shoulder, whispering the special holiday menu as he read. It was impossible to ignore the man, especially when his hand found its way between my thighs.

"The Reindeer Feed is just overpriced Chex Mix, but the Cheesy Snowballs actually sound good," he said nonchalantly, like he wasn't cupping my pussy under the table.

Cheesy...Snowballs?

"The what?" I asked, convinced I had misheard him.

Nixon pointed to the item on the special menu while his other hand drew little circles over the fabric of my thong. How he expected me to focus with the distraction was beyond me.

"Cheesy Snowballs. They're fried balls of white cheddar mac and cheese," he explained as he discreetly moved my thong to the side and slipped a finger inside me. "We could use some real food if we're going to keep drinking. The last place didn't have shit for food."

"That's because it was a wine bar. They don't serve a full menu, just little things like charcuterie boards," Kylie stated.

"It was a nightmare," he corrected.

I wanted to make a witty remark about Nixon being uncultured, but I couldn't form the words. My brain was preoccupied by the finger slowly thrusting in and out of my pussy.

"At least the decor didn't involve dead animals. Putting Santa hats and garland on deer busts and whatever the fuck they did to that rabbit doesn't scream jolly Christmas to me," Quinn said with a grimace.

"Jackalope," I announced, bringing all eyes on me. *Fuck.* The last thing I needed was the entire table watching me.

"What?" Quinn asked.

I swallowed, trying to ignore the finger slowly thrusting inside of me. The smart thing would have been to keep my mouth shut and not draw the attention of the entire group while Nixon fingered me under the table, but hearing Quinn talk about the jackalope like it was a monstrosity made me react without thinking.

"The rabbit with the antlers is a jackalope. It's a mythical animal that inhabits the western parts of America. Poppy loves them," Nixon explained.

My lips drew into a tight smile as I nodded slowly. I was both grateful and irritated that he could carry a conversation so easily when I was desperately fighting a whimper.

Deep breaths, Poppy. Deep breaths.

"Yeah. They are pretty popular decorations in cowboy themed steakhouses," I said with a tight smile.

"Americans are weird," Rupert muttered.

I had a biting insult on the tip of my tongue, but then Nixon slipped a second finger inside of me and all thoughts vanished.

Chapter 14
Hand Check

Poppy

What was the protocol for getting fingered in a country bar surrounded by your unknowing friends? I'm sure it was "don't do it," but I didn't have much of a choice in the situation unless I wanted to make a scene.

You did agree to free use, I reminded myself. As if I could have predicted this was how I would end up.

"Hello, y'all. Welcome to Spruce!" The server greeted us with a thick Southern accent that bordered on fake. *Great.*

Glancing around the table, my friends all wore various expressions of cringe as they each nodded along. At least I wasn't the only one, I guess.

"My name is Jasper, and I'll be taking care of you this evening. Are y'all here for Santa's Naughty Little Bar Crawl?" he asked with far too much enthusiasm.

"He sounds like you when you're really mad," Nixon whispered in my ear.

That was not true. I sounded nothing like that fool. Growing up in Central Florida, I had no fucking accent, and he knew it. At most, I might use the occasional y'all, but that was it.

Nixon's fingers briefly picked up the pace, forcing me to swallow a moan instead of arguing back. Was he riling me up on purpose just to throw me off kilter while he finger banged me under the table? Diabolical.

"Yes, we are here for the bar crawl, but I think some of us wanted to order some food, too," Kylie said, taking the lead.

Thank God. I was in no condition to speak for myself, and Nixon seemed to be in the mood to fuck with me—figuratively and literally.

"Okay. So a round of The Naughty List for the table. Anything else?" Jasper asked, pen and pad in hand.

Everyone gave their orders, Nixon speaking for the both of us as I gripped the edge of the table as inconspicuously as possible. It was hard to sit still and not moan in pleasure. How the fucker was able to act so casual was beyond me. It wasn't like this was something he did frequently. At least, not with me.

As if sensing my turmoil, Nixon leaned forward and nuzzled my neck.

"Relax, Pops. It's Christmas Eve," he whispered like everything was normal. *Asshole.*

As if I could relax. I was being driven to ethereal bliss in public and I couldn't fully enjoy it unless I wanted to risk getting kicked out, if not worse. *Kiss fancy dining and dancing on New Year's Eve goodbye.*

Glancing around the table, I seemed to be the only one aware of what was going on. To my left, Nixon was somehow carrying on a perfectly normal conversation with Kylie, who seemed genuinely oblivious. On the right, Percy and Rupert were explaining the finer points of rugby to Quinn and Mari. Poor Percy had no idea the reason the girls were hanging on every word was because of a manga they started reading recently that centered around the sport.

And you're getting fingered in a restaurant, the little voice in my head reminded me. Like I could forget.

I was close, surprisingly close. It was probably because we were fooling around out in the open and nobody had a clue. As fucked up as it was, the thrill of it made the whole thing ten times as exciting. *You really are a pervert, Poppy.*

In an attempt to appear somewhat normal, I turned to face Kylie, pretending to listen to whatever she was discussing with Nixon. In truth, I didn't register a thing she said. All my focus was on not moaning in ecstasy as I teetered on the edge of blissful insanity.

The crest of the wave was in reach, edging closer and closer. My muscles began to tighten as I prepared to dive headfirst into my release only to have it abruptly ripped from me at the last possible second.

Nixon's hand froze, though he didn't release me. I tried to shift in his lap, a desperate attempt to create the friction I needed, but his other hand dropped to my hip. The bruising grip was a silent warning that I had no choice but to obey. Apparently, the name of the game was edging. *Great.*

I sucked in a sharp breath, schooling my expression. Unfortunately, I caught the attention of Mari, who tilted her head as she studied me—her eyes silently asking if I was okay. I gave her the best smile I could muster and waved her off, not able to explain the frustration I was currently feeling.

What would I even say? *Don't worry. It's nothing. Just Nixon denying me orgasms. No big deal.* Yeah, that would go over swimmingly.

Thankfully, Mari turned back toward Quinn and the rugby players, leaving me to suffer alone.

I didn't have long to pout before the drinks arrived. Each glass had a gingerbread man resting on whipped cream atop a creamy-looking beverage. The festive looking drink seemed innocuous on the surface, but there was a faint whiff of something familiar.

Cautiously, I picked up my glass and took a small sip. Before I could process the unpleasant taste assaulting my tongue, Nixon slipped his fingers back inside me, causing me to choke on my drink.

"Are you okay?" Mari asked. The crease in her brow said she wasn't going to let it go so easily this time.

"She's fine. She just hates eggnog," Nixon answered.

Eggnog? *Fuck.* I had been so distracted by Nixon's handiwork that I missed the putrid taste on my tongue. My face instantly soured as I placed the glass back on the table and pushed it away.

I loved pretty much everything about Christmas—except eggnog. It was the one thing I could never get into, even though I loved egg custard.

"Oh my God, I love eggnog! I'll finish your drink for you," Kylie offered.

Not waiting for an answer, she reached for my drink. Nixon smacked her hand away as soon as her fingers grazed the glass, causing her to curse as she recoiled.

"If anyone is getting her drink, it's me," he announced.

Unlike me, Nixon absolutely loved eggnog. As soon as it started showing up in grocery stores, he'd be stocking our fridge. He could easily drink a half gallon a week by himself during the holiday season, which was good since I hated the stuff.

"You really don't like eggnog?" Percy asked like it was truly a shocking revelation.

"What? A lot of people don't like eggnog," I said defensively. Or maybe I was on edge because Nixon's fingers kept changing tempo, making conversations nearly impossible.

"But this isn't straight up eggnog. There is definitely some ginger in here. I thought you were obsessed with holiday spices," Quinn said.

I picked up my glass and took another small sip, this time focusing on the actual flavors. *Nope, still not my thing.* Putting the glass back on the table, I then grabbed the gingerbread man and used him to scoop off the whipped cream.

"Not my thing, but I'll gladly take the cookie," I replied.

Then I lifted the little gingerbread man to my lips and slowly licked off the whipped cream.

The reaction around the table was mixed. Mari and Quinn rolled their eyes before returning to their conversation, both far too used to my behavior to find it shocking. Percy cleared his throat, uncomfortable by my little performance. Rupert scowled, naturally. Kylie was the only one who looked enticed by the action...until she caught Nixon's eyes behind me.

A small smile tugged at my lips as she sullenly muttered "nevermind" under her breath and looked away. I didn't have to see him to know he was staring her down with a possessive glare.

"Be a good girl," Nixon growled softly into my ear.

The rhythmic pumping of his fingers slowed once again in warning. It was an empty threat. If the name of the game was edging, then it didn't matter how good I was.

"Or?" I asked before taking another bite of my cookie. If my release wasn't going to come anytime soon, why not push back a little?

Chapter 15

Punishment in the Ladies Rooms

Poppy

I didn't have to look at Nixon to know he was glaring at me. He never liked my bratty side. It was one of the few reasons I never considered pursuing anything past friendship. I was a brat by nature. I loved pushing buttons and being put in my place.

It wasn't that Nixon couldn't handle that part of me. He was a great brat tamer, though begrudgingly so. Deep down, my bestie was a cuddle puppy. He needed lots of physical contact, sexual in nature and otherwise. To get what I wanted out of him took a bit of prodding, usually in the form of annoying him past the point of return.

"Excuse us for a moment," Nixon announced to the table. *Bingo.*

His hand slipped from between my thighs and grabbed my wrist with enough force that I knew I was in for some fun. Or possibly a stern talking to, which would suck. *Fingers crossed for the fun option!*

Kylie scooched out of the booth, letting us slide out behind her. I let Nixon drag me along, trying to hold back the giddy smile that desperately wanted to break free. Mari and Quinn both snickered, no doubt thinking the same thing I was—Poppy's getting laid!

Nixon dragged me through the growing crowd of patrons toward the restrooms. I noticed substantially less empty tables than before. My heart began to beat faster as I realized what I had gotten myself into. A little bathroom nookie in an empty restaurant was one thing, but a busy place meant we were more likely to get caught.

Cold feet set in as I tried to slow my steps and pull away. Nixon wasn't having any of it. He dragged me all the way to the restrooms.

"Listen, Nixy, I—"

Before I could finish, Nixon pinned me to the wall next to the ladies' room. His mouth crashed over mine in a frenzied claiming that made my panties melt. I reached out, grasping his sweater in my fists and let him take all he wanted and more. When he finally broke for air, we were both panting messes.

"You're mine. Stop putting on a show for the whole damn table." He all but growled the words.

"Jealous much?" I teased.

Nixon narrowed his gaze, staring at me in silent contemplation. The attention made me shift uncomfortably as I released my hold on his sweater. I couldn't get a read on his expression. Was he genuinely pissed or just fucking with me?

"I'm sorry, Nixy. I wasn't trying to pick a fight," I said, hoping to ease some of the mounting tension.

Nixon's lips curled into a smirk as he straightened his posture and took a step back.

"I know, Pops. You're just being you...but sometimes you drive me absolutely insane," he replied.

I stared at him in disbelief. There was no way I was getting off that easy. His words said I was forgiven, but the look in his eyes said something very different.

Hesitantly, I smiled and gave him a pat on the chest.

"Glad we got that settled. Let's get back to the others so you can continue to tease me under the table," I said.

Turning, I tried to head back to the table, but Nixon placed his hand beside me on the wall, blocking my path.

"Not so fast," he warned.

I froze, my expression faltering for only a fraction of a second before my smile returned. Nixon was clearly messing with me. I couldn't give him the satisfaction of a reaction.

"What? Are you going to punish me?" I taunted back.

He stroked his chin, his head nodding side to side like he was giving my question serious consideration. *Yeah, right.* I knew better than to get my hopes up.

I loved the occasional handprint on my ass, but Nixon was particular about the when's and why's for impact play. As brazen as he'd been so far, spanking me in public was the line.

"Sure. Why not?" he said, surprising me.

Nixon grabbed my wrist and pulled me into the empty restroom. My heart raced with a mix of excitement and fear as he bent me over the nearest sink and lifted my skirt.

My fingers dug into the porcelain as I mentally prepared myself for what was about to happen. I was so damn sure that Nixon was going to turn my ass red, but he leaned down and kissed between my thighs instead.

"Fuck," he whispered as he stared at my pussy from behind.

I watched his reflection in the mirror. His expression was one of both hunger and wonder. How many times had this man seen me naked? And yet he still acted like it was the most amazing sight every single time.

It was a risky move—taking me into a room that was anything but private. There was no way to lock the main door, meaning someone could walk in and catch us at any moment, but Nixon didn't care.

He slowly ran a finger down the small, damp piece of fabric I called a thong. Biting my lip, I tried to muffle my whimper. Then, in an unexpected move, he dropped to his knees behind me. I gasped as I felt his warm tongue stroke me over the lace.

My breathing picked up as I tried to make sense of what was happening. I thought he was going to fuck me, and maybe he still planned to, but the way he was teasing me with his mouth caught me completely off guard. I thought I was going to be punished, but this was nice. No, it was way better than nice.

A moan slipped past my lips as I let my muscles relax. Closing my eyes, I let the anxiety melt away as I fully surrendered to pleasure.

Nixon hooked his fingers under the straps of my thong, slowly peeling it down as he continued to lick me into submission. I was halfway to total oblivion when I felt the thong tug at my ankles. Somehow, I collected myself enough to step out of the garment without toppling over—a feat that was more difficult than I wanted to admit.

Finally free of my thong, I spread my legs, giving Nixon easier access. He gave me one final lick before returning to his feet. I stared at his smug grin in the mirror, my mind muddled by the sudden lack of pleasure.

"What the fuck?" I snapped, more than a little irritated.

Nixon calmly placed my thong in the pocket of his jeans, his expression taking on a neutral tone. He then walked over to the sink next to me and turned on the water.

"If I let you come, then it wouldn't have been a punishment," he stated as he carefully rinsed my arousal from his face and hands.

All I could do was stand there and watch him like an idiot. The asshole had actually bested me.

Our eyes met in the mirror, my expression still one of utter disbelief. Nixon shook his head in amusement.

"Don't give me that look. I'll let you come...eventually," he said.

"Ass." It was the only word I could form in my frustration.

"Yes, but you love me. Now let's get back out there. I want to knock this whole thing out as quickly as possible so I can get you home and take my time," he said.

Nixon then grabbed my hand and led me out of the restroom just as a small group of women in their twenties entered. I ignored them as they gave each other knowing looks, far too busy sulking to care.

Chapter 16
And Then There Were Two

Nixon

I wrapped my arm around Poppy as she cuddled into my side on the couch with a warm cup of the aptly named Whipped on Christmas in hand—our final drink of the night. The boozy whipped cream that topped the hot chocolate really tied the drink together.

We were actually on our second round, our stamp cards turned in a good twenty minutes ago. As much as I grumbled about the bar crawl, the atmosphere at The Triple C was cozy, making it easy for Poppy to convince me to stick around for a second drink. The cuddles didn't hurt, either.

"I had no idea a coffee-house-slash-bar was a thing," Poppy said with a smile on her face.

She let out a content sigh as she lifted her drink to her lips. I followed her lead, taking a sip out of my own mug. The Irish cream blended heavenly with the milk chocolate of the hot cocoa. As much as I hated to admit it, I was having a good time.

"Me either, but I love it," I replied.

The vibe of the place was definitely more coffee house than bar, which was probably why I was enjoying it so much. The overhead lights were dim. Little tea lights sat on the tables, providing a more intimate environment. The plush couch where Poppy and I were nestled all cozy was next to a crackling fire that added to the homey ambience. Even the Christmas playlist, something off one of those lo-fi channels online, made me feel warm and fuzzy.

"I wonder how the others are enjoying themselves," Poppy mused before taking another sip.

I held back a frown, not wanting to think about the others. Honestly, I was relieved every time the group got smaller. Not that I didn't enjoy hanging out with our friends, but ever since we moved from Florida, Christmas Eve night was about Poppy, me, and the traditions I'd adopted because of her.

Rupert was the first to break from the pack, getting a second round at Spruce when a couple other members of his rugby team stopped by. Percy opted to follow us to O'Malley's, but then bailed when Quinn decided to call it an early night. The poor guy was barking up the wrong tree, but he'd figure that out eventually.

Mari ran into some other friends when we got to Sparkies and invited them to join our table, to my dismay. They were a friendly group, but at the time I was itching to finish the damn stamp card and head home, not make new friends.

"I'm sure everyone is having a blast," I replied.

"Even Kylie?" Poppy asked.

She looked so damn worried I couldn't help chuckling.

"Especially Kylie. You saw the way she was flirting with Mari's friend—the guy with the eyeliner and Krampus hoodie. She's having the night of her life," I said.

Poppy let out another sigh, this one more wistful.

"You're right," she conceded.

I could tell there was more on her mind by the way she stared at the poinsettia sitting atop the little coffee table in front of us. Her expression was too pensive to be thinking about that Elmo and Patsy song she loved so much. Something was up.

"Spill it," I said as I gave her a little nudge.

"It's nothing, just the booze," she insisted.

That was fair. We drank a lot in a short amount of time. Honestly, I was a little shocked I wasn't feeling more than a solid buzz. *Maybe that's where all the warm and fuzzies were coming from.*

"What was your favorite drink of the night? I know it wasn't The Naughty List."

Poppy made a low hum as she contemplated the question.

"Probably a tie between this and the drink at the last place—Comin' Down My Chimney," she said.

"Really?" I asked, unable to hide my surprise. "I thought for sure Cockin' Around the Christmas Tree would have been up there."

Poppy shook her head.

"I know I'm not a huge bourbon drinker, but the cranberry juice and cinnamon made Comin' Down My Chimney really good," she explained.

"Ah. Well, I liked the Lick o' the Peppermint Stick at O'Malley's. In fact, I think I liked it more than The Naughty List," I said.

Poppy pulled back from my hold, raising her free hand to her chest as she feigned shock.

"Is Nixon choosing peppermint over eggnog? Really? I never thought I'd live to see the day."

Her voice took on a sweet, southern tone that was slightly exaggerated. It was a common occurrence when she drank, though pointing it out usually turned into a fight. I had no idea why. I always thought the hint of twang was cute.

"Whatever," I said with a roll of my eyes. "If you can enjoy bourbon over wine, then I can like peppermint."

Poppy tilted her head and smirked.

"I feel like that sounded less lame in your head."

Looking down at my mug, I frowned, suddenly worried the booze was having more of an effect than I realized. *Maybe I shouldn't have ordered a second round.*

"Hey. None of that. No frowning on Christmas," Poppy scolded.

Repositioning herself, she crawled into my lap while trying not to spill her cocoa. Once settled, she was curled against my chest, humming along to the music between sips. The moment was perfect. Well, almost perfect.

"Maybe we should wrap it up. We've got plenty to drink at home if you want to keep the party going," I suggested.

"Hm?"

Poppy looked up at me, her lips parted slightly. My mind immediately went to all the naughty things I wanted her mouth to do. I could tell the exact moment she felt my cock waking up by the incredulous look she flashed me.

"Really, Nixy?"

"What? I have a beautiful, sexy woman sitting on my lap. Can you blame me?" I asked.

She pretended to think for a moment before flashing me a bright smile.

"Fine, but I'm finishing my drink first," she informed me. Then, as if to prove her point, she took the daintiest sip possible.

"That's fine. I can wait," I replied. I was the master of waiting.

Chapter 17
Losing Control

Nixon

I was, in fact, not the master of waiting. Most of the ride home was spent sucking face in the back of a stranger's car while the driver made very awkward conversation with themselves. It was probably an attempt to dissuade us from getting hot and heavy in their car, but I wanted Poppy way too much to give a damn.

We broke apart long enough to hop out when the car pulled into our driveway, only to reconnect in a fury of passion. Lips locked, hands roaming in desperation—it was a wonder we made it to the front door.

"Hold up, Nixy," Poppy protested weakly, barely pulling away to speak.

I trapped her bottom lip between my teeth and bit softly, enjoying the way she whimpered in response. Everything about her was so damn perfect. I couldn't fathom stopping for even a second.

Brushing her hair behind her ear, I moved my attention to her neck, alternating between kissing and sucking on her soft flesh. Raw need pumped through my veins, my body burning despite the chill of the cold winter night. I needed to be naked, my rock hard cock thrusting inside her wet pussy, and I needed it now.

"I—fuck—I need to get my keys, Nixy. Give me a second," she pleaded, her voice a husky, lust-filled whine.

"No," I said, nipping her neck for emphasis.

"Nixon—" she continued to protest, much to my annoyance. Why was she being so insistent?

"I said no! I don't want to stop, Pops. I need you so bad. I'll fuck you right here, under the stars, if I have to."

A sharp sting radiated from my scalp as Poppy grabbed me by the hair. She yanked my head back, holding me in place with her firm grip.

"It is too damn cold to be fucking outside. Now stand here and wait while I unlock the door, okay?"

"You agreed—"

"I'm going to stop you right there, Nixon Aiden Collins. We both know nothing is going to happen unless I allow it, and I am not allowing a damn thing to happen until we are inside where it's warm. Unless you prefer to handle things alone, you're going to behave," she said, her voice even and full of authority.

Fuck. Why did that turn me on even more?

"Yes ma'am," I replied.

Poppy smiled as she leaned forward and placed a chaste kiss on my lips. It took everything in me to stand still. The need to feel her cunt squeezing my cock was almost too much to ignore, but there was also pleasure in drawing out the anticipation and giving someone else control.

"That's a good boy," she said.

Releasing her hold, Poppy rummaged through her purse as she stepped toward the door. My eyes tracked her every movement under the soft, colorful glow of the Christmas lights strung along our home's exterior. I longed to reach out and touch her, but I knew better. My time to be in charge was over. Poppy was in control now.

The lock clicked, and my cock wept with joy. Poppy opened the door, taking two steps past the threshold before turning to face me.

"Are you coming?" The way she placed a hand on her hip and stared back at me expectantly made a smile cross my lips.

"Soon I hope," I replied softly while smiling.

Poppy smirked, shaking her head in amusement as she turned and continued farther into the house.

"Come along," she ordered when I didn't immediately follow.

With renewed excitement, I rushed inside, barely stopping long enough to close the front door behind me. My need had been building ever since we started the bar crawl. Fingering her cunt had been meant to be a tease, something to make her want to rush home and be with me, but it backfired spectacularly, making me just as needy.

Tasting her in the bathroom at Spruce certainly didn't help matters, either. My dick took forever to go back down after that.

"Clothes off, Nixy. I want you naked and on the couch," Poppy called out from the living room.

Fuck yeah!

I eagerly undressed, leaving a trail of discarded clothes behind me as I rushed to join Poppy in the living room. My skinny jeans proved to be more of a fight than I anticipated. Poppy sat naked on the couch, laughing as I hopped and grunted my way across the room.

Frustrated, I dropped to the ground and rolled onto my back, legs in the air. Poppy's laughter grew louder, but I didn't care. The position was necessary if I ever wanted to be free of my pants.

Once they were off, I jumped back to my feet and removed my boxer briefs. Standing naked and proud, I waited a beat for Poppy to calm before joining her on the couch. Despite the minor setback and being laughed at, my erection was still at full mast. Nothing was going to deter me from ending the night with a bang—literally.

Not wasting any time, Poppy straddled me. The feeling of her tits pressed against my chest was almost as heavenly as the warmth of her wet cunt on my lap. I wanted nothing more than to sink my fingers into her soft ass, holding her still while I slipped my dick inside her.

Patience, Nixon. She's calling the shots.

"You were a naughty boy tonight," Poppy said, her voice dripping with lust. "Fingering me in public like that, what were you thinking?"

I smiled at the memory of stretching her pussy while surrounded by our friends. Not a single one of them had any idea what was happening under the table.

"You enjoyed it," I replied.

Poppy narrowed her eyes as she stared me down.

"My enjoyment wasn't the question," she scolded.

"It's the only thing that matters," I countered.

She pulled her bottom lip between her teeth as she tilted her head to the side. It was all an act—pretending she wasn't pleased with my answer—meant to make me squirm a little. If I didn't notice the spark of excitement in her eyes, I probably would have believed it.

Placing her hands on my shoulders for support, Poppy leaned down and nipped at my ear. The sensation made my muscles tense as goosebumps erupted over my body. She was toying with me, and I loved every second of it.

"I'll keep that in mind," she whispered, her warm breath caressing my skin.

Then she gripped me by my hair and yanked my head to the side, exposing my bare neck. Before I could react, I felt the sharp sting of her teeth biting into my flesh. I let out a cry that faded into a moan as she began sucking on the spot.

"Please," I whimpered, my hips thrusting involuntarily. "I need to be inside of you. Please, Poppy."

She released my skin with a pop, making me whimper all over again.

"Begging already?" she mocked.

"Yes!" I was well past the point of pride. My cock was so stiff that it bordered on pain. I needed to fuck, and I needed it now.

Thankfully, Poppy was willing to put me out of my sweet misery. She reached down and grabbed my cock at the base, holding it steady as she lined herself up with the head.

Relief washed over me as she slowly slid down my shaft. Without any real prep, it was a tight fit, but that didn't stop her. She continued past each piercing until I was nestled fully inside her.

I don't know how long we stayed like that while she acclimated to my girth. Time lost all meaning. All that mattered was Poppy and I were one.

When she finally started moving, I felt overwhelmed. To be so close, our bodies pressed together as she rode me, was more than I could handle.

"Fuck. You feel so good. You always feel so damn good," I praised between moans. I wanted her to know—no, I needed her to know she was perfect. Nothing could ever compare.

Poppy was a vision riding my cock—her head thrown back as she moaned, pleasure overtaking her. She was close, but I was closer. If I didn't do something, I was going to finish before her and I couldn't let that happen.

Reaching around, I slipped a hand between her ass cheeks, pressing a single finger against her tight ring of muscles without actually penetrating her. The reaction was instant. Her nails dug into my shoulders as a high-pitched squeal of ecstasy poured from her.

The walls of her cunt fluttering around my cock as she drowned in her orgasm was my breaking point. I let out a strangled moan as euphoria crashed over me. My chest tightened, my whole body stilling as I filled her perfect pussy with my cum.

By the time I came down, I was breathless and dizzy, barely able to keep myself upright.

Chapter 18
A Christmas Eve Confession

Nixon

Christmas jammies were a longstanding tradition in Poppy's family. Everyone got one gift to open on Christmas Eve—the pajamas you were to wear that night. Even though we were adults in our thirties living states away, Fran still sent us our Christmas jammies.

The awkwardness of being included in a family tradition that wasn't my own had long since faded. I told myself it was part of moving on and healing. My parents may not have wanted me, but Poppy's did. Dave and Fran loved and accepted me for who I was.

This year's Christmas jammies theme was onesies, much to Poppy's delight. The way she shrieked with excitement when she opened the colorfully wrapped box and pulled out what looked more like a costume than sleepwear made me laugh. The Krampus onesie felt very Poppy and she agreed, immediately stripping down and putting it on.

My reaction was much more subdued when I opened my Spider-Man onesie, but I was no less appreciative. Fran definitely knew her kids. Feeling included amongst them made me feel all warm and fuzzy.

After a brief call to Fran and Dave to give our thanks and promise to call again Christmas morning, we snuggled on the couch and started the final Christmas Eve tradition—watching *National Lampoon's Christmas Vacation*.

The first time I watched the movie was my first Christmas Eve with Poppy's family. None of them could believe that I made it to my twenties without seeing it. I didn't know how to explain that my parents found no entertainment in the plight of the common man, so I made up some vague excuse about overly strict parents and prayed they didn't push it further.

If you had told me that night that fourteen years later I would be sitting on a couch with Poppy's head in my lap while we watched Clark Griswold slowly descend into madness, I would have thought you were crazy. (And not just because I had no idea who Clark Griswold was at the time.) Yet here I was, living the dream.

"Randy Quaid's bulge," Poppy murmured as she pointed to the actor on the screen.

Another tradition that was solely Poppy's was to point out Randy Quaid's obvious bulge during the scene where he cons Clark into buying his kids' gifts for Christmas. I chuckled softly, loving that something so ridiculous could bring her so much joy.

"Laugh at him, not me. I can tell the difference." She pouted, though her words were barely audible. *Someone's tired.*

"I'm not laughing at you, Pops. I'm amused. Your dorky humor is adorable. It's part of why I love you."

I paused, realizing how good it felt to say those three little words. For once, I wasn't afraid of the consequences. The last month was amazing. Every month going forward could be just as great if I stopped being scared and took the chance to lay it all out there.

Before I could talk myself out of it, I decided to take the leap and confess my feelings.

"And when I say I love you, I mean it. You're my everything, Poppy. You're the person I want to spend the rest of my life with. You're my forever, my soulmate. And I think if you'd give me the chance, I could make you as happy as you make me."

I let out a breath, the relief of finally putting that out there washing over me. I was free and now all that was left was Poppy's response.

My heart constricted as the seconds ticked by with no response. Panic started creeping its way through. Had I ruined everything after all?

The sound of soft snoring cut through the mounting tension like a knife. I held back a bitter laugh as I realized my confession fell on deaf ears, or rather sleeping ones. Oh well. There was always the morning, assuming I didn't lose my nerve by then.

Turning my attention back to the movie, I let myself get lost in the whimsical world of the Griswolds as Poppy slept on my lap. For now, this was enough.

About the author

Lizzie spends her winter days sipping red wine by the fire while crafting the perfect fictional men for her readers. Her summers are spent exploring the PNW with her family and taking her dogs to the nearby dog park. She has an extensive collection of tokidoki figures that are in no way alarming. It took around two decades to acquire what she has, and is a point of pride. The figures are a much safer topic of discussion than the growing number of pillow boyfriends she has procured.

Learn more about Lizzie and her works at <u>https://lizziebbrown.com</u>.

Also by

Lizzie B Brown

The Holiday Pact:

Friendsgiving with Benefits
Coming for Christmas

Obedience:

Obedience Volume One
Obedience Volume Two